# THE HEIRESS AND
### *the*
## COWBOY CONTRACTOR

## Maggie Carpenter

Copyright © 2023 by Maggie Carpenter

Published by Dark Secrets Press
Ebook Cover Design
Dark Secrets Press LLC

## PROLOGUE

Nicole Harris looked every bit the wealthy young woman she was. Her long hair was perfectly styled, thick red lipstick matched the red bra peeking through the expensive white silk shirt, and the red porcelain beads gracing her neck. But she was furious.

Clenching her fists in frustration, she was standing in what should have been a finished kitchen, complete with quartz slab countertops, a picture window overlooking the lake below, and dark hardwood floors. Instead she was staring at plywood beneath her feet, a counter that was nothing but a frame, a huge empty space where the window should have been, and trash scattered everywhere she looked.

Not only had her dream house become a nightmare, in a few minutes she'd have to face Beau Chapman, the local contractor she'd refused to speak with several months before.

When she'd started the project, her longtime friend, Helen Meyer, who had a vacation home in the small lakeside town, had done her best to persuade Nicole to meet with him but Nicole had said no, and as she surveyed the mess she grimaced as she recalled the conversation.

"I'm telling you, he's terrific," Helen had insisted. "Why would you want to use some city contractor when there's a guy here who knows the people and the community? He'll be able to get things done. He knows who to schmooze. Besides, the people here don't like outsiders coming in and—"

"You can stop right there," Nicole had interrupted. "I'm not having some dirt kicking, blue-jeaned, straw-chewing horse trainer as my contractor. I want someone good, someone who knows what they're doing. Your friend might be able to repair a fence, maybe even put up a barn, but my contemporary vacation home? I doubt it."

"At least talk to him. I've already told him you'd be calling. Please? You won't be sorry. Besides, he's total eye candy."

Nicole had flatly refused, but now she had no builder, and her house looked like a modern-day ruin. Feeling backed into a corner she'd finally agreed to call the guy the locals referred to as the cowboy contractor. He'd been cordial on the phone, almost friendly, but it was clear he hadn't forgotten the brush-off.

Hearing the sound of tires crunching up the gravel driveway, she hurried off to meet him, her high-heels clip-clopping as she walked. But in her haste she failed to see the half-empty bag of cement laying in her path. With a wail she fell forward, her arms flailing in the air, but miraculously her hands hit a support beam. Clinging to the pole as she caught her breath, it was only when she straightened up she realized what she'd done. Pulling off her black pump, she scowled at the high glossy heel hanging by a thread.

"How fucking annoying is this?"

Continuing to curse under her breath, she pulled off its mate and dropped the shoes on top of the cement bag, then continued forward in her stocking-feet. Reaching the patch of earth where the deck should have been, she grunted as she stared down at the loose ground. It looked impossible to walk over.

"I can't let him see how desperate I am," she muttered under her breath. "I can't believe it's come to this. Some dopey cowboy my last hope."

As the truck rolled to a stop, she noticed the sun glinting off polished chrome, and the turquoise paint was as glossy as glass. Unexpectedly feeling a jolt of nerves, she moved her oversized black sunglasses from the top of her head over her eyes.

The driver's door opened. The first thing she saw was the cowboy hat. Light tan and sitting forward on his brow made it difficult to see his face. As he stepped from behind the door, she couldn't believe how shockingly white his shirt was. Then she saw his jeans. They fit perfectly, as though he'd worn them a thousand times. Raising his head, to her dismay he was wearing reflecting aviator glasses.

"Hey there, you must be Nicole Harris."

He was approaching the wide patch of dirt, and as he neared she scrutinized him. Square jaw, ruggedly handsome features, broad shoulders, and she guessed he had a stomach she could wash her clothes on. Her girlfriend was right. He wasn't just eye candy, he was the whole damn box of chocolates.

"Good to meet you. I'm Beau Chapman. I think you'd better start by tellin' me what's happenin' here?"

His voice matched. Thick, and deep, and he spoke with a drawl.

"You mean what isn't happening here," she quipped. "It's a joke, one big fucking joke."

"Huh," he muttered, walking through the dirt, his dark brown cowboy boots paying it no heed. "Looks like what you said on the phone. Someone just up and left, and it looks like a while back."

"How can you tell?"

"The amount of dust over everything for a start, cobwebs—"

"Cobwebs!" she exclaimed, cutting him off. "Where? I hate spiders."

"Yep, see up in the corners?" he pointed, walking past her into the house. "I'd say it's been at least a couple of months, maybe longer."

"You're wrong, it's been—"

"Nope, I'm not wrong."

"I'm not good with time," she said vaguely, "and I've been busy. This is the first chance I've had to come up here. I told you that when we spoke."

"Hmm, well I'm tellin' you, Miss Harris, it's been a whole lot longer than a couple of weeks," the cowboy remarked, ambling into a massive space that was supposed to be the living room.

"I don't care," she said sharply. "I just need to know what I'm looking at."

"What you're lookin' at is a mess," he replied turning to face her. "There's a lotta cleanin' up to do before I could even get started."

"Oh, for fuck's sake, I know it's a mess!"

She had followed him, and standing about ten feet away, she felt awkward and oddly self-conscious in her stockinged feet. As he slowly removed his sunglasses she felt an unpleasant churn in her stomach. Even before they were all the way off, she spied a frown—then his eyes. Smoky blue and captivating.

"So," she continued brusquely, refusing to show any weakness, "when can you start and how much is it going to cost me?"

"I haven't agreed to work for you yet," he said, his mesmerizing gaze making her swallow hard, "and I'm not sure I'm gonna."

"Excuse me?"

"I said, I haven't—"

"I heard you, I just don't understand."

"This is what I suggest," he drawled. "You find yourself a builder who doesn't mind you speakin' to him like a lackey, and who isn't particular about bein' called by their name. I'll bet the two of you will get along just fine, but me, I'm leavin'."

He'd delivered his soliloquy in a monotone, his eyes never leaving her dark glasses, as though he could see right through them. Suddenly he was marching past her. Panic-stricken she turned to catch up, but he was traveling at a quick clip.

"Fuck, would you wait a minute?"

"Nope."

"Wait," she called again, "can we start over?"

* * *

Already across the patch of dirt and heading to his truck, Beau Chapman was insulted and angry, but not just angry with her. He was angry at himself for making the trip. She hadn't been warm and fuzzy during their phone call, but in person she was downright rude, and had the mouth of a drunken sailor.

He'd reached his truck and was about to open the door when a shrill cry pierced the silent, still air. Spinning around he saw her laying on the filthy plywood in her pristine white suit, her head thrown back, wailing in shock.

Sprinting across the drive and through the dirt, he leapt up the step and hurried to her side. Dropping quickly to one knee, he put an arm around her shoulder and tried to sit her up.

"Easy now, easy. Tell me what happened."

"M-my f-foot. It's, oh, f-fuck, it hurts."

"Take a deep breath and try to calm down."

"N-not sure I c-can d-do that."

"I'm gonna take a look."

Already suspecting what had happened, he gently released her, then moved down the length of her body to study the soles of her feet. The sight wasn't pretty. Swallowing his reaction, he moved back to her side.

"Miss Harris, I need to carry you into my truck and get you to a doctor."

"Is it bad?"

"Looks like you stepped on a nail," he said smoothly. "Be better if a doc saw to it. You need an x-ray before it gets...uh...removed."

"Ooh, it's so painful. Just t-take m-me to m-my hotel. Hillsboro."

"Sorry, but you're goin' straight to a doctor. I'm gonna lift you, okay?"

"C-can we take my c-car? M-my stuff is in there."

He'd noticed the Lexus SUV when he'd arrived, and she was right. It would offer a more comfortable ride than his pickup.

"Sure, yeah."

Carefully scooping her up he carried her through the dirt and across the driveway, but as he settled her into the passenger seat, she began panting and moaning loudly.

"Try to slow your breathin'."

"Okay. Thanks s-so much for not leaving m-me," she stammered. "I'm s-scared."

"You're gonna be just fine, and no way would I leave you. Damn, girl, what kinda people are you used to dealin' with? Let's take these off," he suggested, reaching for her sunglasses.

Worried that she'd fallen into shock, he needed to study her eyes. Carefully lifting the glasses off her face, it was immediately apparent under the thick red lipstick and heavy makeup was an attractive, but frightened and vulnerable young woman.

"I...uh...feel a bit f-funny," she bleated. "C-cold. Really c-cold."

"I have a blanket in my truck. I'll be right back. Don't worry, you're just in shock, but I need to keep you warm."

As he sprinted across to his truck, he pulled out his phone and called one of his buddies. The man also happened to be his doctor.

"Should I take her to emergency or to you?" he asked, picking up the blanket and jogging back to the Lexus.

"Bring her here. I don't want her sitting around in a waiting room, and I'm closer than the hospital. "

"Got it, thanks, Hank."

He'd reached her car, and dropping the phone back into his pocket, he placed the blanket around her, but his worry grew. She was white, and she gazed at him with a vacant expression.

"I'm takin' you to my doctor. He's not far. You'll be fine."

Running around the car and jumping into the driver's seat, he said a prayer of thanks the key was sitting in its holder on the console. Driving carefully down the gravel driveway, he shook his head. Life was full of surprises, and glancing across at her, he had the strongest feeling he was at the beginning of something, though what, he had no clue.

# CHAPTER ONE

In the waiting room of Dr. Hank Gilbert's office, Beau stared absently out the window. Though the view offered a delightful scene of the lake across the street, he didn't see the children playing, or the joggers, or the dogs being walked. He was racked with guilt.

If he hadn't been so quick to march away, Nicole wouldn't have hurt herself, and he couldn't blame her for being frustrated and angry. Some asshole had left her high-and-dry.

"Beau?"

Turning around, he saw Hank holding the door that led back to his examining rooms, and Nicole hobbling out on crutches. Her long brown hair fell softly around her shoulders, and though her clothes were dirty and her makeup smudged, he was taken by her beauty.

"Fortunately it wasn't a two inch nail," Hank declared. "I've given her some antibiotics and pain medication, but she needs to lay down and stay off that foot for a couple of days. She'll be fine, but she's had a nasty shock."

"You're a lifesaver, Hank, thank you," Beau said gratefully. "I'll make sure she doesn't go anywhere. Come on, Miss Harris. I'll get you back to your hotel."

"I'm staying at the Hillsboro Suites," she murmured. "I'll pay for a cab to get you back to your truck."

Her voice was quiet, and he didn't like her color. She was still white.

"So you mentioned," he said as they moved slowly through the waiting area.

"I did? When?"

"Back at the house."

"I don't remember. Anyway, I'll pay for a cab."

"Don't worry about that, not for a minute," he said firmly, holding the door open for her.

"I insist."

"Insist all you want, but it's still not gonna fly," he insisted, as they made their way down the hall. "You need to—"

"I don't need anything," she muttered, cutting him off, "and you don't have to worry about me. I'm fine."

They'd reached the elevator, and moving inside she leaned against the wall and closed her eyes.

"You're about as fine as a rainy day," he softly drawled.

She didn't answer him, and when the doors opened, he held his hand against them so they wouldn't close.

"Sit down and wait here. I'll bring the car around."

"No, it's okay, I can manage."

"You don't need to manage a dang thing. Sit yourself down and wait for me. I'll be right back."

"But I—"

"But nothin'. You're as white as a sheet. Now do as you're told and sit your butt down."

She stared at him, and he suspected it was rare for her to be challenged, but to his relief she surrendered and sank into a chair.

* * *

Grimacing in pain as she watched him stride across the parking lot, she cursed herself for being so rude when he'd arrived at the house. He was sexy as hell and ruggedly handsome. A far cry from the men she'd known throughout her life, especially the current, unwanted man. Gerald! She scowled just thinking about him.

Her Lexus pulled to the curb, and she struggled to get back on her feet, but as soon as she was upright she was hit by a wave of dizziness. She stood for a minute, hoping it would pass, but it didn't, and she flopped back down.

"Hey, are you all right?"

"How did you get here so fast?" she mumbled, looking up at him.

"I'm just outside."

"I saw the car, but I didn't see you get out. I guess I went a bit funny, but I'm fine."

"Quit sayin' that," he declared, and before she could respond, he'd picked her up and was carrying her to the car.

"Put me down. This isn't necessary. I said I'm fine."

"You can say that as many times as you want, but it's not gonna make it true. You're not fine. I saw you virtually pass out. Nobody faints then walks away on my watch," he said firmly, managing to open the passenger door and placing her gently into the car. "I'll fetch your crutches."

Leaning back, she knew he was right. She felt light headed and her foot throbbed. With no energy or desire for small talk, when he returned and slipped behind the wheel, she barely glanced at him. As he drove from the parking lot, she stared through the windshield and remained quiet, but as they made their way to the hotel, she felt him constantly glancing at her.

"Why do you keep looking at me?"

"Miss Harris—"

"You can call me Nicole."

"Nicole, I'm just guessin' here, but have you eaten today?"

"What?"

"It's almost two-o'clock. Did you have lunch, or even breakfast?"

"I had...uh...some coffee at the hotel, and then stopped for a latte on my way to the house."

"No wonder you're gettin' dizzy. Two cups of coffee on an empty—"

"Latte is all milk."

"Wow, a cup of hot milk, that'll keep you goin'," he retorted, rolling his eyes.

"I got here late last night and I was still a bit tired this morning. It was a long drive, four hours. I was too wiped out for anything but coffee."

"You should have your butt spanked!" he muttered under his breath.

"Excuse me?" she exclaimed, staring at him in shock. "What did you just say?"

"Askin' like that, I'd say you heard me!"

They'd reached her hotel, and she lowered her window to get some air. A hot flush was suddenly crawling through her body. Pulling to a stop and jumping from the driver's seat, Beau threw the keys to the valet. As the young man grinned and gave Beau the parking stub, Nicole spotted an attractive young woman with a wide smile hurrying forward pushing a wheelchair.

"Hey, Beau."

"Hey, Amy, thanks for this."

"Anything for you," the girl twinkled. "Where's the patient?"

"In the car. Where do you think?" he answered with a chuckle, walking quickly around the SUV.

It was obvious Beau was known there, and as the girl followed him and moved the wheelchair into place, Nicole summoned her best smile.

"Nicole, this is Amy," Beau said, opening the car door. "Amy, this is Nicole Harris."

"This is so nice of you," Nicole said gratefully, "but how did you know I'd need help?"

"Beau called us," the perky girl replied. "If you need anything at all, just call the front desk and ask for me, or Roger, he's the manager."

"You got any of that chicken-vegetable soup today?" Beau asked as he helped Nicole into the chair.

"Sure do."

"Send up a big bowl with some bread, and a pot of tea with honey. Dessert as well. She hasn't eaten since yesterday," he finished, taking the handles of the chair and rolling it forward.

"Sure thing, Beau, and I'll grab the crutches from the car."

"I am here," Nicole mumbled.

"What about you, Beau? Can I get you anything?" Amy asked, still batting her eyes at him.

"I had lunch at Nate's, but I'll take some tea."

"A cowboy who drinks tea? Now I've heard of everything," Nicole quipped.

"I learned all about tea from a friend who stayed at my ranch for a while. She got me hooked."

"I'll just bet she did."

If he'd heard the comment, he chose to ignore it, and as they made their way into the hotel, Nicole turned around and looked up at him.

"Why are you being so nice to me? I wasn't exactly friendly when we met."

"You're a damsel in distress," he replied, pushing her into the elevator. "What's your room number?"

"Three-seven-four."

It was a short trip to the third floor, and not sure what else to say, she remained quiet as he rolled her down the hallway.

"Here we are," he declared, stopping at her door.

"Shit. My bag. I left it in the car."

"Don't worry, Amy will be right behind us, she can let us in—and there she is already," he said, looking down the passage. "Hey, Amy. That was fast."

"I took the stairs," Amy said breathlessly as she reached them. "Here are your crutches, and I saw your purse on the floor of the front seat so I took the liberty."

"You're an angel," Beau said gratefully. "Thanks, hon."

As Nicole watched the brief exchange, she felt a twinge of jealously. No-one had ever called her an angel. Not even close.

"Here you go, Miss Harris," Amy said with a smile as she placed the bag on Nicole's lap. "I can let you in."

Amy used her master card to open the door, then held it open as Beau wheeled Nicole into the room and across to the bed. Lifting her from the chair and gently laying her on the bed, she let out a heavy sigh.

"That feels so much better. Thank you."

"You're welcome."

Leaning the crutches against the wall, Amy began pushing the chair away, and Beau followed to hold the door.

"Thanks so much, Amy. Has the food been ordered?"

"Yes, it won't be long. Let me know if she needs anything else—or you do—anything at all."

"Amy, I've already told you," he said softly. "I'm too old for you."

"You really mean I'm too young."

"It's the same thing."

With a dramatic sigh, she pushed the chair into the hall, and shaking his head, he ambled back to Nicole and sat on the side of the bed.

"How are you feelin?"

"My foot hurts like hell, but at least I'm here," she muttered, then fixing him with a steady gaze, she said, "You didn't answer my question. Why are you helping me when I was so—?"

"Rude and obnoxious?"

"Yeah, I guess."

"It was partly my fault."

"Why?"

"You were totally stressed, and I don't blame you. It's a rotten thing for a contractor to do, leavin' you in the lurch like that, and it probably didn't help bein' strung out on caffeine."

"Yeah, I was really wired."

"I should've just let you complain. Normally I would. Normally I'm a very patient man."

"Yeah, I kind of get that. So, why weren't you?"

"Probably 'cos I was at a bar with some guys celebratin' last night, and I woke up with a hammer in my head."

"I know what that feels like," she said grimly. "What were you celebrating?"

"It was for a friend of mine who's—" but before he could finish there was a loud knock. "That'll be room service," he declared, standing up to answer the door, "and I'm stayin' to make sure you eat."

In spite of the pain in her foot, and feeling like she'd been hit by a truck, as he strode to the door, she found herself wondering what it would be like to have a man in her life as caring and as strong as he was.

"Why are you lookin' at me like that?" he asked, rolling the trolly to her bed and lifting the tray.

"No reason," she replied, trying to think of a way to ask if he was attached.

"Uh-huh."

"Amy seems like a sweet girl. She's got a mad crush on you."

"I know. If I was younger, or she was older, I might be interested. Anyway, are you comfortable? I'm gonna put this on your lap."

"Yes, I'm comfortable," she replied, propping a pillow behind her back. "Don't you have somewhere to be?"

"The only place I need to be is here."

"That's a big bowl," she muttered, staring down at the soup. "I don't usually eat in the middle of the afternoon."

"Am I gonna have to flip you over and spank your butt to make you eat, 'cos I will if I have to?"

The hot flush she'd felt in the car abruptly returned. Moving from her belly into her chest, then over her neck and crawling across her face, it left behind a bevy of butterflies dancing a dance she'd never felt.

"Uh, you, uh, you shouldn't say things like that."

He didn't answer, and though she'd dropped her eyes, she could see his lips curl into a wicked grin.

"What about my house?" she asked, wanting to change the subject as she picked up a spoon.

"When I go back to pick up my truck, I'll take another look," he offered, sitting in a nearby chair.

"I'd appreciate that, and this soup is amazing. Thanks for arranging for it, and, uh, everything else."

"All part of the service, ma'am," he said with a chuckle. "We didn't get off on the right foot, and—"

"I sure as hell didn't," she exclaimed, interrupting him.

"Sorry, bad choice of words."

"It was the perfect choice of words," she replied, thinking she was almost glad she'd stepped on the nail. "Speaking of feet, would you mind collecting my shoes while you're there?"

"Be happy to, and the color's comin' back to your face."

"I have to admit this soup is helping. I still feel a bit light-headed, but you were right. I was starving, I just didn't know it. Tell me about this town. What should I know?"

He chatted as she ate, and though she pretended to pay attention, all she could focus on were his thick, moist lips, and wondering how it would feel to be wrapped up in his powerfully muscled arms. When she'd finished and he stood up to leave, she was determined to find out.

## CHAPTER TWO

The following morning, after a delicious breakfast and a call from Beau saying he'd be there in half-an-hour, Nicole wrapped a plastic shower cap around her bandaged foot and managed to take a shower. The hot water streaming over her body was a slice of heaven, but as she dressed and applied her makeup, she prayed he hadn't tracked down her former contractor, though she suspected he would have spoken to the obstinate man at the city.

Her room was a semi-suite and offered a living area that overlooked the lake. Making sure the door to her room was unlatched, she hobbled to the couch and put her leg up. As she waited, gazing out at the view, she felt a wave of desperation.

"He has to agree to finish my house, he has to. There's nobody else," she muttered grimly. "I've burned too many damn bridges!"

The knock on the door startled her, and sending a last minute plea to the heavens, she called for him to come in. The look on his face was not encouraging.

"You look so serious," she remarked as he walked over and sat in a chair opposite her.

"How's your foot?"

"The pain pills help."

"Another day or two it should be feelin' better."

"I hope so. That's what your good doctor said, but what about the house? How much will it cost, and can you do it? Will you do it?"

"Before I give you my answer, you need to tell me why your last contractor bailed."

Her heart sank.

"Why do I think you've already spoken to him? I suppose you're going to believe every nasty thing he said about me."

"I asked you why he quit. That means I'm willin' to hear your side of things."

"We didn't get along. Can we leave it at that," she asked, trying not to sound defensive. "I really don't care to go into the sordid details."

"Then I'm not sure we have much else to talk about," he declared, rising from his chair.

"Wait, please."

"Are you gonna tell me what happened?"

"Yes, I will, it's just—I hate postmortems."

Sitting back down, he crossed his ankle over his opposite knee, took off his hat, and stared at her. His wavy black hair fell over his forehead, giving his smoky-blue eyes an almost mesmerizing effect.

"I'm waitin'," he drawled, snatching back her attention.

"It's quite simple really," she managed. "I wanted him to do certain things to the house and he refused."

"Because?"

"Because he claimed the city wouldn't agree. I told him to do it anyway. I figured once the place was finished it would be so gorgeous the city wouldn't care, but he wouldn't listen. It was so fucking frustrating," she exclaimed, suddenly throwing her hands in the air. "He said he'd face fines, but I told him I'd pay the stupid fines, then things got really heated and he quit. I gave him a check for what I owed him and that was the end of it."

"What about the city? What happened with Daniel Walters?"

"Daniel Walters? How can you work with that man? He's so stubborn!" she said with a scowl. "I went down there myself. I told him my house would be the pride of the community. He heard me out, I'll give him that, but then said I couldn't build my house the way I wanted. I thought this was a free, fucking country."

Her frustration had bubbled over, causing her voice to rise in pitch and in volume. Watching her, Beau was reminded of a little girl throwing a tantrum.

"That's quite an angry streak you've got," he remarked, suppressing a grin.

"Wouldn't you be angry?"

"Seems like you don't have any trouble tellin' people what you think," he replied, ignoring her question. "Would I be right about that?"

"Absolutely."

"I'm curious. Would you mind tellin' me how can you afford such an expensive home?"

"I happen to be the Marketing Director of Pantera Jeans," she said proudly. "You've probably heard of them."

"Sure, who hasn't. I might be just a simple cowboy, but seems to me it'd take a whole lotta years to climb the ladder and reach such an important position."

"I...uh...my grandfather founded the company. I've worked there my whole life. When I graduated college I decided I wanted to be in the marketing side of things, and it just so happens I'm exceptionally good at my job."

"That sure explains a whole helluva lot," he said with a nod. "Yep, surely does."

"I work very hard!"

"Yep, no doubt."

"So—are you going to help me with my house?"

"Nope."

"I don't understand. What's wrong with you?"

"Sugar, there's nothin' wrong with me," he said quietly, dropping his foot from his knee and leaning forward in his chair. "The something wrong is on your end. I said you don't have any trouble sayin' what you think, so I'm gonna give it right back. You are a spoiled, self-centered little girl who needs her butt spanked, just like I said yesterday."

"How dare you!" she retorted, but even as she protested she could feel the infuriating heat ripple through her body.

"You may be a Princess in your grandaddy's company, but here you're just a slick city girl comin' in and tryin' to make something happen we don't want."

"This makes no sense," she argued, trying to ignore the butterflies that had joined the prickling heat. "Why wouldn't you want a gorgeous home here?"

"Take a look around this town, Nicole. Whatta ya see? Cozy cabins, homes that have been here for decades and lovin'ly cared for. Sure, we've got some big houses, but they're not concrete and steel and chrome. The city has a buildin' code for many reasons, and one of those is to maintain the integrity of this place."

"Haven't you ever heard of progress?"

"Yep. Hey, we've even got cell phones," he quipped, "but there's only so much progress we're gonna allow here, and honey, that house of yours, that ain't gonna happen."

"Fuck!"

"That's another thing. Your momma shoulda washed out your mouth a long time ago."

"I can't believe you're saying these things," she muttered angrily, but taking a breath, she stared out the window, wondering why he had such a profound effect on her.

"Just callin' it like I see it, but gettin' back to your house, I'm surprised you got as much done as you did. You wanna tell me how that happened?"

"May as well. I paid some of the contractor's guys under the table to do some work he hadn't authorized. I thought at some point he'd buckle, or that Daniel guy at the city would buckle."

"You can't be that naive," he said incredulously. "Did you really think that would work?"

"I saw my dad do it once. In the end he got everything he wanted."

"That won't happen here. We're gonna keep our town as perfect as we can, for as long as we can."

"My dad always says never to surrender," she said firmly, "and I've seen how effective that can be."

"There are times when surrenderin'," he said slowly, lowering his voice, "let's just say, it can be the best choice."

She didn't respond, and leaning back in his chair he glanced out the window. It was a beautiful day, yachts were skimming across the lake, kites were dancing in the air, and when he got home he was going to take Pepper, his big grey quarter horse, out for a ride. He suddenly felt sorry for the spoiled heiress sitting in front of him.

"Nicole, life here is simple, and it's good," he began. "The kids can play in their front yards, dogs can run loose around the lake, I can ride my horse in the hills. It's slow-paced and easy. This might not be the place for your second home."

Turning his eyes to hers, his mind unexpectedly flashed back to the moment in the car when he'd removed her sunglasses. She'd been in pain, but that aside, he'd sensed a vulnerability, almost a sadness. He unexpectedly wondered how much of her attitude was just her way of protecting herself.

"So, that's it?" she mumbled, her voice suddenly quiet. "You won't talk to Daniel whats-his-name at the city?"

"Nope, I agree with him."

"Fuck."

"Why do you use language like that? It doesn't suit you."

"It's how I feel. I want my house. I'm frustrated and angry."

"No-one's sayin' you can't have your house. You just can't have it exactly the way you want it, or you can, but somewhere else."

"I like it here. This is where I want to be."

"Then change the house so it conforms to the city's code."

She paused.

"Beau, will you build it for me if I do?"

"Wow, you really are relentless."

"Is that a yes?"

"I think you—"

"Beau, please," she suddenly begged. "I know I'm a bit difficult, but I really need this house."

There was desperation in her voice, and for the first time he sensed there was more to her story than just a rich girl wanting a vacation home. Much more.

"I'll tell you what I'll do. I'm gonna have a friend of mine call you. His name is Geoff. He's an architect. The two of you can meet during this week while your foot's healin'. If you play nice with him—"

"Play nice?"

"You gonna let me finish?"

"Sorry, sorry, yes, go ahead."

"If you play nice with him, and you come up with something that'll work, hopefully without havin' to tear down too much of what's been done, then you and I will have another talk, but..."

"But? There's a but?"

"Yep. That talk is gonna happen at my ranch. You're gonna come out and spend the day with me and my horses."

"I've never been around horses," she murmured with a soft smile. "I'd really like that."

"In about a week your foot will be better, and I'll know if you've behaved yourself with Geoff. If you've been a good girl, you'll come out to the ranch and we'll take it from there."

"Why do you speak to me like I'm ten years old?"

"Maybe you should think about that question," he replied, rising to his feet. "Call me if you need me, and I mean that, otherwise, maybe I'll be seein' you in a few days."

"I'd walk you to the door but—"

"Don't even think about it," he said, putting on his hat. "You've gotta let that wound heal. I'll catch ya later."

As she watched him saunter across the room, she felt an unfamiliar tugging at her heart.

"You have a good day too," she called after him, wanting him to stay.

He turned and touched his hat, then was gone.

"Who are you," she muttered, "and why are you making me feel this way?"

Sighing deeply she shifted her gaze back to the lake.

"Whatever this Geoff guy says, I'll be Miss Goody Two Shoes," she murmured. "I can always change things later. Yeah. I've got this. No problem."

# CHAPTER THREE

As the days ticked by, Beau received only glowing reports about Nicole from his architect friend. She had listened attentively as he'd explained the construction guidelines, and when they started discussing the modifications of the existing plans, she'd liked his suggestions. By midweek it seemed things were falling into place, and Beau received a call from Geoff with his report.

"She wants this house built yesterday, and she totally understands she can't have a large contemporary," Geoff declared. "She's accepted every one of my ideas. I can't remember any client being so cooperative. They always have something they want to change."

"That all sounds encouragin', but let's see where you are at the end of the week. She might suddenly do a one-eighty on us."

Hanging up the phone, Beau fought the temptation to call her. His instinct told him to wait, but it wasn't easy. He was worried about her foot, and he was concerned she wasn't eating enough. Later that night he found himself wanting to drive to the hotel, knock on her door, kiss her like crazy, then turn her over his knee and spank her until her bottom turned scarlet.

The next couple of days seemed to drag, and though he was busy with ranch work, she remained in the forefront of his mind. He was in his barn saddling his horse when Geoff called and told him he and Nicole had signed an agreement. Beau felt a wave of relief, but he caught himself. It was still early days.

"She's given me a check," Geoff declared. "It's happening, Beau. We're ready to move forward. I've spoken to Dan and we're meeting up tomorrow."

"That's good news," Beau replied. "Let's get together at the hotel around six tonight, then I can say hello to her when we're done."

"Works for me. I think you'll like what we've come up with."

"Hey, as long as it's legal and she can live with it, I'll like it. Thanks for lettin' me know. I'll see you later."

Ending the call, he turned to the big, grey gelding.

"How about them apples?" he muttered, stroking his horse's neck. "You think this crazy woman has seen sense?"

As if he understood Pepper snorted, then shook his head.

"I agree, fella. I'm optimistic, but that's it. A leopard doesn't change his spots that quick, but at least she's behaved herself, and I reckon she's earned a call."

\* \* \*

Nicole was preparing to go for a walk. Her foot had healed, and it only occasionally reminded her she'd stepped on a nail.

She'd spent her days talking to Geoff and discussing the changes to her house, then falling asleep in front of the television in the evenings. To her surprise, she'd enjoyed amazingly deep sleep, and a chronic ache she'd carried in her shoulders had virtually disappeared.

Venturing out to amble across to the lake, though she pondered profound thoughts about her life, her mind always took her back to the cowboy contractor. Settling on one of the benches and gazing across the lake, she was thinking about taking a stroll when her phone rang.

She knew it was him. She didn't know how she knew. She just did. Her pulse quickening, she answered the call.

"Hello?"

"Nicole, it's Beau."

"Hi Beau. How are you?" she asked, his deep, sexy voice bringing her butterflies to life.

"I'm fine, how are you? How's the foot?"

"The foot is almost like new. I'm up and around. Thank you so much for putting me together with Geoff. He's a genius. My house has been salvaged."

"He said you two were gettin' along. I'm glad to hear it. I gotta say, you sound like a different woman."

"I do? Huh. I guess I was pretty stressed."

"You must've needed a break, and I'm pleased you liked Geoff's ideas."

"He was so easy to understand," she continued. "I'm really excited, and I can't wait for the work to start."

"I'm meetin' him for a drink around six to take a look at the sketches. Would you like to have dinner afterwards?"

"I would love that, yes, definitely," she said enthusiastically. "Should I just come down? Do you want to eat here at the hotel?"

"Seems like a plan. Meet me in the restaurant at seven. An hour with him should be long enough."

"Fantastic, and Beau?"

"Yeah, Nicole?"

"Does this mean you'll be my contractor?"

"It means we're havin' dinner, and you're comin' out to the ranch."

"You're tough."

"I don't make promises I can't keep. One step at a time. Dinner, then the ranch."

"I'm really looking forward to that. I've been thinking about it all week. I really am thrilled. I've always wanted to spend time around horses."

"Be a good girl at dinner and you might even get to sit on one."

"Oh, my gosh," she breathed, wondering why she felt the strange, but wonderful flip in her belly when he called her a good girl.

"Do you have a pair of comfortable jeans and boots?"

"I'll get some today," she said quickly. "To be honest, I may work for a big-time jean company, but I don't wear them very much."

"There's a store in town called Wally's Western Duds. Turn right outta the hotel. It's just a couple of blocks down. You can't miss it. Tell Wally I sent you. He'll make sure you get what you need."

"Thank you! I will."

"I'll see you soon."

"Yes, see you soon," she replied, and ending the call, she dropped her head in her hands. "What the hell? You're a cowboy! I can't believe I'm feeling all this for a fucking cowboy."

Straightening up, she stared at her reflection in the mirror. The forced week of rest had done wonders.

"I do feel better, a lot better," she murmured, "and I think this house might actually get built."

* * *

Beau had ended the call with a wry grin.

"Well, Pepper, that was interesting. If I didn't know better, I'd be thinkin' I've misjudged her," he said, leading his horse into the yard.

Placing his foot in the stirrup, he swung himself into the saddle, and as he headed towards a trail that would take him around the lake, two completely separate images of the wealthy heiress floated into his head. The arrogant, tailored city woman who had spat at him from behind large dark glasses, and the injured, vulnerable girl that had gazed up at him sitting in her car after the accident.

"A brat and a beauty," he muttered as his horse walked calmly down the trail. "I know why you're a brat. You've been handed everything on a silver platter, and I'll bet you're a nightmare to work for. Damn. As much as I wanna help you, and as much as I wanna spend time with you, do I really wanna take this on?"

The day was warm. Puffy cotton clouds drifted aimlessly across the sky, and approaching the lake he stared up at the hill where the unfinished house could be clearly seen.

"That is one ugly sight," he grunted. "Yeah. I'm gonna take the job, and make sure it's done right. If she gives me a hard time, I'll put her over my knee. Hell, I'll put her over my knee anyway. She needs that attitude spanked outta her, and I don't believe it's gone, not for a minute. Let's face it, Pepper, she just needs to be spanked good and proper, period."

He could see it so clearly.

Seated on a hay bale in the barn, her bared backside turning a bright pink as he slapped her perfectly round cheeks.

"I'm gonna spank you hard, girl."

The image sent his cock to life.

Turning Pepper into a thicket of trees, he slid from his saddle, and leaving his horse to happily graze, he quickly unzipped his jeans and leaned against a tree. Wrapping his fingers around his engorged cock, he closed his eyes and pictured the scene.

*She was wearing a white cotton dress and sandals, her long auburn hair tousled from the wind that was blowing off the lake. They were standing in the front of her new house on a redwood deck. Moving tentatively forward, she stopped in front of him, lowered her eyes, mumbled an apology, then bent over.*

His climax was building fast.

He paused, lifting his gaze to the glassy water.

It was serene. A living postcard.

Catching his breath, he closed his eyes back down and continued to stroke his rampant cock.

*Wrapping his arm around her waist, he lifted her dress and found lacy white panties. His hand slapped down, leaving his bright red handprint on her curvaceous backside.*

A sudden wave of prickling tingles rocketed through his limbs. With his manhood exploding across his hand, he let out a series of deep groans, but the climax ended as abruptly as it had begun.

Sighing heavily, he slid down the tree and sank into the grass. Shards of sunlight beaming through the branches kissed his face. He could have drifted off for five minutes, but taking a breath, he reached into his pocket to grab his kerchief.

"Damn girl, what the hell?" he muttered as he wiped himself. "I can't believe I stopped to do this. Why do I think you're gonna be trouble even if you do behave?"

## CHAPTER FOUR

When Nicole walked into Wally's Western Duds, her mouth fell open. She had never seen such a huge selection of clothing, and it was all western wear. Dressed in her cream pressed slacks, pink silk shirt and high-heeled cream sandals, she felt distinctly out of place. An attractive man she guessed to be in his forties, wearing a twinkle in his eye and carrying a swagger in his step, wandered over to greet her.

"Hi there. I'm Wally. Anything I can help you with?"

"Hi, yes, you can. I'm a friend of Beau Chapman's. He's going to put me on a horse. I've never ridden and he suggested this was the place to find what I need."

"Beau? Then you get my gold star service," he grinned. "Let's start with jeans and a shirt, then the boots. The boots are real important."

"I own a ton of boots."

"I doubt you've got the kind you'll need," he remarked. "What's your budget?"

Wally always asked, and even though Beau's new friend wore a Cartier watch and designer clothes he made no assumptions.

"I'm not too worried about that, but whatever I buy I'd like it to be versatile."

"You mean, you wanna wear the clothes some place other than a ranch."

"Yes, exactly."

"The jeans I'm gonna suggest are tapered and stretchy."

"That sounds good. I know all about jeans," she said with a grin.

"Come on over here and I'll show you which racks to check out. When you're ready to start tryin' on, the dressin' rooms are easy to see. Just look for the doors with the mirrors on the front."

Escorting her to the jeans section, he offered a few suggestions, then pointed out the brands he preferred.

"Wally, Beau's been extremely helpful and I'd like to buy him something to say thank you. If you think of anything he might like, or need, would you let me know?"

"You bet. I'm sure something will come to mind."

After an hour of trying various jeans and shirts, Nicole was finally satisfied, and when it came to the right footwear, Wally recommended paddock boots.

"These will give your foot stability in the stirrup," he explained. "You can spend all day in them and they'll still be comfortable."

When they were finished, and she stared at herself in the large mirror that hung on the back of the dressing room door, she was elated. The stretch blue jeans hugged her curves, and tapering into the ankle-high black boots, they gave her legs length and accentuated their shape. The white and red check shirt was snipped in at the waist, but the lycra blend fabric offered plenty of give.

"I love this look," she murmured. "It's sexy, and talk about flattering!"

"Knowin' Beau he'll wanna put a helmet on you, but I think you need the finishing touch," Wally declared.

Walking quickly across to a display of western hats, selecting a white one with a red band, he hurried back to her and popped it on her head.

"There ya go! You look pretty damn sharp," he exclaimed, cocking his head to the side. "If Beau hadn't beaten me to it, I'd be invitin' you out to sit on one of my horses."

"I love the hat. It's perfect, and I want another pair of these jeans in black, and this shirt in aqua, and the pink shade as well."

"You want me to wrap up your other clothes?"

"No thanks. I'll change back into them. Did you think of anything for Beau?"

"I did. When you come to the counter I'll show you what I've got in mind."

As she slipped back into the dressing room and peeled off her new clothes, she sighed happily. Everything was falling into place. She'd soon be sitting on a horse for the first time, Beau was going to build her house, and she was sure they'd become friends.

"Hopefully more than friends," she murmured. "Of course I'll have to deal with Gerald! Fuck. That won't be easy, but I have to do it. I have to make it official."

As she left the dressing room with the jeans and shirt draped over her arm, she paused, and turning around she looked at herself in the cream slacks, pink silk shirt and high-heeled sandals.

"Ick, talk about boring. I think I'm going to change my look, at least when I'm here."

Striding across to the counter, Wally began placing her purchases in a garment bag.

"While I'm doin' this, why don't you take a look at what I found for Beau? He'd be tickled to get any one of these."

"This one, and, yes, that one too!" she exclaimed, pointing to her choices. "This has been so much fun. Thank you, Wally. You've been great. I can't wait to visit Beau's ranch and wear all this great stuff."

\* \* \*

While Nicole had been shopping, Beau had returned to his ranch, taken a shower, then called Gina, his housekeeper, who also happened to be one of his dearest friends.

"Could you stop by tomorrow mornin' and cook up your baked chicken? I'm havin' a guest. I'd love to serve it for lunch."

"A guest? I'll be happy to, and I'll make some of my chocolate cheesecake tonight and bring it over."

"That would be great. Thanks, Gina."

Ending the call, he couldn't deny his growing excitement. He was about to drive into town to speak with Dan about the permits, but he had a fleeting moment of panic. Nicole was a city girl. How would she feel about his ranch once she arrived? Would she care if there was manure in the barn? He would have cleaned the barn, but horses were horses.

"I'm bein' ridiculous," he muttered, grabbing his hat and jacket as he headed into his garage.

In addition to his vintage truck, he owned a late model Jeep

Cherokee, a better choice for the evenings. The night air could be nippy, and as much as he loved Betsy, her heater wasn't the best. Driving into town he pushed Nicole's pending visit to the back of his mind, and focused on his meeting with Dan. They'd been friends since they were kids. Dan had been hassled by Nicole and her builder, and Beau wanted him to know, if he accepted Nicole's offer and took over as the contractor, all the hassles and drama would be history.

Pulling into the parking lot he jumped from his jeep, walked into the small building that housed city hall, and poked his head around Dan's office door.

"Do you have time for a humble contractor?"

"Hey, Beau, good to see you. Come on in. Did you get everything worked out with the diva? Geoff's done a great job with the modifications."

"Yep. The house is smaller for a start," Beau remarked. "She was tryin' to put a monster on that lot."

"So, the question is," Dan said raising his eyebrows, "are you going to build it?"

"You're right. That is the question! I'm sure thinkin' about it. What else can you tell me I might not know?"

"Are you aware that she's had it wired to be a smart house? Blink and the lights go on kinda thing."

"No, I didn't," Beau said with a worried frown. "I don't know crap about that stuff."

"Most of the work's been done by an electrical company I've never heard of. I don't see it as a code problem, at least not yet, but it'll be a notch above Lyle's head, that's for sure."

Lyle Brady was Beau's electrical contractor, the best in town, but Daniel was right; Lyle was steak and potatoes, not gourmet French food.

"I'll talk to her about it," Beau said, making a mental note. "Anything else?"

"She didn't get a permit for a pool, but I know it's been staked out."

"I saw that and wondered about it myself. I'm guessin' a geology report would have been done, but it looks dicey to me."

"Like I said, she didn't apply for a permit, and that's gonna take a while. Those are the only things that come to mind, but if I think of anything else I'll let you know. Are you sure you wanna get involved with that woman? She was hell on wheels when she came in here."

Beau paused, leaned back in his chair and smiled.

"To be honest, Dan, I'm lookin' forward to it. Life's been a bit borin' lately, and I don't think that girl has a borin' bone in her body."

"You're one brave cowboy," Dan said with a chuckle.

They shook hands, and as Beau headed back to his Jeep to drive to the hotel, he knew if the owner was anyone but Nicole, he'd probably pass. He didn't need the money, or the early mornings and late nights, but Nicole was interesting, not to mention a challenge.

"The thing is," he mumbled as he drove through town, "just how much of a challenge will she be?"

Swinging into a parking space in the hotel lot, he wandered inside, stopped at the front desk to say hello, then ambled into the hotel bar. Geoff was already sitting at a table with his sketches laid out. Beau settled in, ordered a beer, and began to look them over.

"This is real good, Geoff. I see you left a ton of open space inside, and I'm guessin' that was her idea. Hmm, you've closed in these front walls and reduced the amount of glass."

"I had to," Geoff remarked. "With the winds we get, and the flying debris, those big sliders weren't smart. In fact, they were downright scary."

Beau's eyes were focused on the plans, but something made him lift his eyes and glance across the room. For a split second he thought he saw Nicole walking past the entrance to the bar wearing a white dress.

A shiver pricked his skin.

She'd been wearing what he'd pictured earlier when he'd been leaning against the tree and imagining the two of them together.

"Hey, Beau, are you okay?" Geoff asked. "You look like you've seen a ghost."

"What time is it?"

"Just gone six-thirty."

"I have to check something."

Jumping to his feet, he hurried from the lounge into the wide hallway. Looking up and down, there was no sign of her, or any woman in a white dress. Continuing to the entrance of the restaurant, he peered in. It was virtually empty.

"Hi, Beau," the hostess said, walking up to greet him. "We have your reservation for seven o'clock, but I can seat you now if you want."

"Did my dinner guest arrive? She's wearing a white dress."

"Sorry, I haven't seen anyone in a white dress."

"Huh. No-one came by here?"

"No, not that I saw."

"Okay, thanks. I'll be back at seven."

Shaking his head, and wondering if he'd been imagining things, he returned to the bar.

"Is everything okay?" Geoff asked as Beau approached the table.

"Yeah," he relied, sitting down, "but I need something stronger than beer."

"What's going on? Don't say nothing, because something obviously is."

"I thought I saw Nicole, but I was wrong. Weird though," he mumbled, then suddenly the drunken conversation with Clyde flashed through his head.

*You don't understand, I saw her, but she wasn't there. I mean, like a ghost, like she was so much on my mind I imagined her. It freaked me out, but when I told Pa he said it meant she was the one.*

"Holy crap!"

"What's wrong? Did you just remember something?"

"Yeah, kinda," Beau mumbled. "I think I've got a problem. A big one."

## CHAPTER FIVE

Nervously waiting outside the restaurant, hoping Beau would like the white dress she'd chosen, Nicole spotted him striding towards her. She caught her breath. Dressed in khaki slacks, a light tan and blue checked shirt, and cowboy boots, the rugged cowboy looked even more handsome than she remembered.

"Hi, Beau. I feel like it's been ages," she said, unable to stop herself from leaning forward and pecking him on the cheek. "I'm so happy to see you."

"I'm happy to see you too, and that's quite a welcome. It sure beats the first one you gave me."

"Sorry about that," she replied, feeling a blush cross her face. "I admit it wasn't my finest moment. Are you okay, you look a bit—"

"Yep, fine," he said, interrupting her, "but before we go in, can I ask you something?"

"Sure. You can ask me anything."

"Were you here earlier?"

"Earlier? Of course I was here earlier," she said with a grin. "I'm staying here, remember?"

"I mean earlier, as in, about half-an-hour ago. Did you happen to walk past the bar?"

"No, I came down about ten minutes ago. Why do you ask?"

"I, uh, thought I saw you, but it must have been someone else. That's a real nice dress, by the way. You look very pretty."

"Thank you, I'm glad you like it. You don't look so bad yourself. Almost like a regular guy, not that I don't like your cowboy clothes," she added hastily. "I do, I think they're great, this is just—sorry—I'm rambling."

"You're not rambling. You're just searchin' for words, and forgive me for sayin' so, but bein' sweet looks a whole lot better on you than a cocky attitude."

"Uh, thanks, I think."

"It was meant as a compliment. Are you hungry?"

"I am, and before you ask, yes, I've been eating."

"Glad to hear it. Let's go in," he said, placing his hand on her back.

His touch sent a warm, delicious ripple down her back, and loving the thrill, she walked with him into the restaurant.

"What's a regular guy?" he murmured as they waited for the hostess.

"I guess, not a cowboy, but like I said, I like the cowboy thing. I loved shopping at Wally's today."

"You went there? Cool. Yeah, he's a good guy. I've known Wally a long time."

"Hello again," the hostess said with a warm smile. "Would you follow me?"

Leading them to their table, Nicole realized they were being taken to one of the best spots in the dining room. Tucked away in a corner next to a window, it offered a view of the lighted swimming pool.

"Here are your menus," the hostess declared, handing them the leather folders. "I'll send over the drinks waiter. I hope you enjoy your meal."

"What did she mean by again?" Nicole asked quietly as the young woman walked away. "Do you eat here often?"

"When I thought I saw you earlier, I came by here to check, and no, I don't eat here often, only on special occasions. The food is excellent."

"So, this is a special occasion?" she asked, tilting her head to the side.

"Absolutely, and Nicole," he murmured, leaning across the table. "Regardless of what I'm wearin', I'm still a cowboy underneath."

"I never doubted that for a minute," she replied, thinking his shirt made his blue eyes sparkle like crazy.

Feeling a fresh flush cross her face, she dropped her gaze and reached for the water glass, but as she took a sip, she decided she would kiss him before the night was over.

"Nicole, why did you want me to think your contractor had left you just a couple of weeks ago?"

The unexpected question caught her off guard, and she hesitated, struggling for an answer.

"Don't think about it," Beau said firmly. "Just tell me the truth."

"Must I?" she asked with a dramatic sigh. "Can't we talk about something else?"

"We can talk about anything you want, but only after you answer the question."

"You won't like the answer," she muttered, taking another sip of water.

"Let me put it like this. I'm not likin' not knowin'. Bein' lied to doesn't sit well with me."

"Okay, Beau, the fact is I spent weeks trying to get someone else and everyone said no. They were either too busy, or didn't want to work so far out of town, or their subcontractors were tied up. There was always some lame excuse. The one company that did agree must have heard I was desperate because they wanted to charge me a ridiculous amount of money. I lied because I didn't want you to know that you were, uh—"

"Last on your list, and your last hope?"

"Something like that, and I also didn't want to risk getting another exorbitant quote."

"First off, my quotes are my quotes, regardless of the circumstances, and second, I already knew you were reachin' the bottom of the barrel. My ego didn't much care for it, but I knew you were from the city and probably didn't have a simple country contractor high on your priority list."

"You knew? But how?"

"When you bought that land and started buildin', you didn't reach out to me for any of the work, but I heard things through my friends in the city, and I watched it go up. I also watched it come to a stop, and sit untouched for weeks, or was it months? You honestly thought I wouldn't have noticed?"

"Oh, yeah. Of course you would have seen it. Sitting on the knoll overlooking the lake and the town, it's hard to miss. Sorry, and I'm also sorry I didn't contact you when I started the project."

"No problem. I don't take it personally," Beau replied, smiling across the table at her. "You didn't know me from Adam, and you still don't."

"I know enough. You saved me, and you totally took care of me even after I was so rude. I don't think anyone's ever been that considerate. Have I thanked you properly?"

"You thanked me plenty, now let's take a look at our menus. I'm starvin'. You want some wine? A drink?"

"Yes, definitely. I've been off those painkillers for a couple of days, so I'm good to go! A glass of Chardonnay would be great."

* * *

Beau found himself enjoying her company, and she'd been straight with him about her contractor problems. Though she still seemed a bit wired, she was more relaxed than he'd expected, and after a glass or two of wine, he hoped the real Nicole would surface. Not the defensive, uptight, entitled woman he'd initially met, but a feminine, happy girl.

Catching the wine steward's attention, he ordered a bottle, then looking across at the gorgeous girl in her white dress and deep green eyes, he couldn't deny the immense attraction. As she let out a sigh and tilted her head to the side, he noticed an unfamiliar look in her eye. The word that came to mind was unguarded.

"You look, different," he remarked. "Good different."

"Thanks, I think," she said softly. "To be honest, I didn't realize how badly I needed a break. I can't remember the last time I did nothing for several days. I don't think it's ever happened before, and I feel as if I can breathe in this little town. I'm not sorry I stepped on that nail, not at all."

"Sometimes things happen for a reason, even the bad things."

"My dad says that we make things happen, and fate doesn't exist. He doesn't believe in luck."

"It that so? Huh. Well, regardless, the rest has done you a world of good."

"You can see it?"

"I sure can. Your eyes, they're softer."

"Wow, that's pretty poetic talk for a cowboy."

"I have my moments," he said with a grin. "Tell me more about Nicole Harris, and I don't mean about your work, I mean about you. If I'm gonna build your house, and I'm not sayin' I will, but if I do, I need to know who I'm buildin' it for. Besides bein' opinionated and stubborn," he said without batting an eye, "tell me about your life. What do you do for fun, what do you love, and what drives you crazy?"

Her reaction was not one he expected. She didn't blush, or sigh, or smile, or begin talking. She looked directly at him, frowned slightly, then the waiter arrived with the wine. Trying not to be impatient, he went through the ritual of tasting and approving, and sat quietly as the waiter poured. When he finally left the table, she picked up her glass and raised it in a toast.

"To new friends."

"I'll drink to that," Beau said, clinking her glass, "and I'll add, I hope we'll one day be good ones."

"Yes," she said emphatically. "I'm sure we will."

They sipped their wine, then he waited, not sure if he should press. Finally setting down her glass, she leaned across the table.

"I'm not sure where to start."

"Wherever you want."

"Well, I'm rich, but you know that, I'm smart, you know that too."

"What don't you like?"

"Crowds, I hate being in throngs of people, or standing in line. I like ice cream too much. In fact I love anything creamy, and..."

"And?"

"And I'm building a house here because—uh— this is hard to talk about, and I don't know why I'm telling you. Maybe I shouldn't."

A slight frown had crinkled her brow, and he waited as she picked up her glass and took a long drink.

"You don't have to tell me anything that makes you uncomfortable."

"I want to tell you," she said, letting out a sigh. "I'm building the house because I want a new life. I want to be away from the traffic and the noise and the phony, demanding people. I'm building the house because I want to escape. I need to escape. There, I've said it! Fuck! That's the first time I've spoken the words out loud. Look at me, I'm shaking," she exclaimed, holding her trembling hand in the air.

She looked as unnerved as she claimed. Wondering what she was leaving behind that was so terrible, he reached across the table and wrapped his fingers around hers.

"Take a deep breath," he said softly. "That was impressive, and I thank you for tellin' me. I'll bet it's real hard to break away."

"You have no idea," she murmured with a heavy frown. "You have no fucking idea."

"You know what, I'm not gonna call you Nicole. To me, you seem more like a Nickie, though probably a naughty Nickie!"

"Me? Naughty Nickie?" she said, managing a smile. "I guess I can be."

"Yeah, you can, and here's the good news. I will build your house, and if you want, I'll be your friend."

Her face flushed. A wave of emotion was flooding her heart, and gazing into her deep green eyes, he sensed she was beginning to open up. He was real, and he believed she knew she could trust him.

"That would be wonderful, if you would be my friend, I mean."

"But there is one condition, Nickie," he said softly, squeezing her hand, "tonight, after we have dinner, I'm gonna spank you."

# CHAPTER SIX

Though Beau hadn't meant to say it, he'd certainly thought it. The words had rattled through his brain the moment Nicole had started drinking her wine, and her green eyes had gazed at him over the rim of the glass. For a fleeing moment he'd believed the promise had remained just that, a thought repeating itself loudly in his head. But her eyes had widened, and she'd looked so stunned, he'd realized the words had spilled from his mouth.

"What did you say?" she whispered.

He stared at her, momentarily tongue-tied. He couldn't take it back, nor did he want to.

"I think you heard me," he managed, "but if you'd like me to repeat it, I will. Is that what you want?"

"Um, I'm not sure," she stammered.

Though still in shock that he'd made such an outrageous suggestion, she couldn't deny she found it frighteningly tantalizing.

"It's not rocket science," he said with a smile, summoning the confidence he'd briefly lacked. "I said, after dinner, I'm gonna spank you."

Repeating the simple statement helped. He felt like himself again. Throughout his life he'd threatened, suggested, hinted, and on more than a few occasions, had yanked the bad girl sharply over his knee without warning, but he'd never sat across a table and made the statement so blatantly to a woman he barely knew.

"Are you serious? I mean, why would you say something like that?" she asked testily. "Wait, are you just joking around?"

Her face had turned beet red, and he suspected the gusset of her panties was moist, very moist.

"If I was jokin' around I'd be laughin', and the why? You mean besides the obvious? Anyone that has the word naughty in front of their name is ripe for a spankin'," he said softly, then leaning across the table and lowering his voice even more, he added, "I did tell you earlier you needed a spankin'. Twice if I recall."

"But, uh…"

"You're right, there is a butt, and as I said, I will spank it after dinner. However, there is a condition."

"A condition?" she squeaked. "What kind of condition?"

"I'll spank you only if you want me to. You can think about it. If you decide it's something you want, you'll tell me."

"If I want? Seriously?" she exclaimed, her face flaming. "How am I supposed to eat anything with that hanging over my head?"

"Nothin's hangin' over your head. You can say no, but not until after we finish our dinner. You'll give me your answer when I walk you to your room."

As she stared at him in disbelief, he reached across the table and took her hand.

"It's okay, we can talk about something else now," he said with a warm smile. "You can tell me about our mutual friend Helen, and I'll tell you a bit about my horses. The mare I'm gonna put you on is called Trixie, and she's a real sweetie. She likes beginners. You won't have to worry. She'll take real good care of you."

"Trixie, what a cute name for a horse," she managed, amazed she could talk about anything with the threat of a spanking over her head.

"She looks like a Trixie," he remarked, "at least I think she does. Sometimes we humans give our animals names that don't suit them at all."

He could see she was quietly freaking out, which meant she was aroused by the suggestion and didn't know how to respond. The best thing he could for her was to remain completely casual, and picking up the menu, he began chatting about the dishes on offer.

* * *

In spite of the growing wetness between her legs, and the fluttering butterflies in her stomach, Nicole was able to maintain her composure, but as the meal continued she found herself aching to feel his lips brush against hers. She was also conflicted by a dire fear attached to a confusing desire to be spanked.

Their meals were served, and as they ate, she managed to chat about how she'd met Helen at college, and how much she was looking forward to seeing his ranch and sitting on a horse. The food was delicious, and for a few precious minutes she forgot about Beau's wicked threat, but when their plates had been cleared, and the dreaded moment was at hand, she took a deep breath and leaned over the table.

"I seriously cannot believe you said that to me," she said in a hushed whisper.

"Said what, exactly?"

"You know. About the spanking thing."

"It's not a thing," he declared with a devilish grin. "It's a spanking. My hand, your butt."

"Must you keep saying that?" she retorted. "I mean, for fuck's sake."

"Why do I have the sneaking suspicion you've made up your mind, and in spite of all your squawkin', you want me to spank you?"

"What if I said no?"

"Then I'd walk you to your door and say goodnight."

"That's it? No drama?"

"Not from me. I'm not into drama. Are you sayin' no?"

She paused.

"It's either yes or no," he pressed, "or do you need more time?"

"Maybe I should tell you what I'm thinking?"

"If you want, but I can guess."

"You can? Okay, what am I thinking?"

"You're thinkin' something like this. *What's wrong with me? I really want him to spank me, but I don't.* How's that? Am I close?"

"Yes, you're close," she muttered, staring down at her hands.

"Tell me, Nicole, what is it about being over my knee that scares you?"

"Everything," she replied with a heavy sigh.

"You need it," he said solemnly, "and there's a part of you that knows I'm right."

"Then it must be keeping quiet," she mumbled, still not lifting her eyes.

"You can't lie to me about this," he said, his self-assurance unnerving her even more. "You do need it, and you want it for several reasons.

"Like?"

"First, you're a brat, and some of that brattiness has to be spanked out of you, but tonight wouldn't be about that. Tonight would be about helpin' you calm down a bit, and understandin' that you can let go."

"Fuck."

"And I will definitely spank your ass for swearin' all the time. Take this as a promise. The next time you use that word, I will swat you—hard—and it won't matter where we are."

Her head jerked up.

His smoky-blue eyes made her heart skip.

Heat sprang between her legs and burned her face.

"Would you excuse me for a minute?" she said quickly, pushing back her chair.

"Of course. I'll order us something delicious for dessert."

She could feel his eyes on her as she rose to her feet and walked slowly to the ladies room. Though desperately in need of some space to clear her head and gather her thoughts, she believed whatever she decided it would be fine with him. She also believed at some point, that night, tomorrow, the day after, the following week, he would spank her. It wasn't a matter of if, but when, and they both knew it.

Brushing her long dark hair and applying a fresh coat of lipstick, she took a deep breath and left the ladies room. Looking across to their table, she saw the waitress hand him the small leather folder listing the decadent desserts on offer.

A strange sensation rippled through her body.

Though she wasn't sure why, she felt compelled to say yes.

As the realization floated into her head, he looked up and caught her eye. She began walking back to him, and as she neared the table, he handed the menu back to the waitress.

"I don't think we'll be havin' dessert after all. Just put the check on my tab and add twenty percent."

"Thanks, Beau," the waitress said with a grateful smile. "It's always good to see you."

Nicole settled into her chair, picked up her napkin and began fiddling with it.

"Beau?"

"Yes, Nickie?"

"I do want dessert, but not that kind. I want the other kind."

"You mean, the kind that I deliver while you're over my knee?"

Lifting her eyes, she slowly nodded her head.

"I don't even know why," she quietly admitted. "I mean, I feel strange even thinking about it."

"You'll soon find out why."

Rising from the table, he took her hand, and helped her up. Feeling slightly unsteady, she was grateful he waited a moment.

"Are you okay?"

"Of course not."

"I wouldn't be snappy if I were you."

The comment sent a fresh wave of butterflies through her stomach, but he gave her hand a reassuring squeeze.

"It's natural to be nervous. I get that, but you can't be rude."

"Sorry."

"Ready?"

"No," she replied with a dramatic sigh, "but we can't stand here all night."

Stepping slowly forward, he led her out of the dining room, and down the long hallway to the elevator.

"This is so weird," she whispered, leaning against his shoulder as they waited.

"It's not, but I know you feel that way," he said softly, dropping her hand to put his arm around her shoulder. "It will be fine. You'll see."

The elevator arrived, and walking inside he hugged her tightly until it dinged their arrival on her floor. Keeping his arm around her, they headed down the passageway, but when they reached the door she fumbled nervously with the card key.

"Let me," he offered, taking it from her hand.

Sliding it into the metal box, the tiny light turned green, and she let out a long sigh.

"Maybe I'm not...um...can I change my mind?" she murmured as they entered the room.

"Of course you can."

"Then, that's what I'm doing," she said breathlessly, wishing she wasn't such a coward. "Thanks for a lovely dinner and, uh, everything."

"You're welcome. I'll pick you up around ten tomorrow mornin'. Be sure to have a light breakfast."

He turned and headed to the door, but as he wrapped his fingers around the handle, she rushed forward and grabbed his arm.

"Beau, before you leave, will you kiss me?"

* * *

He stared down at her.

Neediness danced in her eyes.

Clutching a fistful of hair, he jerked her head back, and dropping his lips to hers he devoured her mouth. Suddenly throwing her arms around his neck, her muffled moans floated like a lullaby in the air. Finally breaking apart, he held her tightly, relishing the feel of her breasts against his chest.

"Fuck, Beau, that was-"

His hand blasted against her bottom.

The thin cotton of her dress had offered no protection, and she stood, motionless, her eyes blazing up at him. Silent seconds ticked by, then purposefully gripping the back of his jacket, she took a deep breath.

"Fuck!"

The second smack was harder.

"Fuck!"

Moving his hand to her opposite cheek he dispatched a volley of three quick, sharp spanks.

"Ow, ow, fuck that hurt."

Her eyes were filled with challenge. Her face bright red.

"Okay, Nickie, now you're goin' over my knee."

# CHAPTER SEVEN

The alacrity with which he strode the few steps to the bed and jerked her over his knee shocked her. For a brief moment time stood still, then abruptly breaking from the spell, she kicked and squirmed as he tried to position her.

"Enough of the histrionics," he said sharply, landing several quick swats.

"Stop! Stop!"

"Yell one more time and you'll find a gag in that sassy mouth of yours. The manager's a friend of mine. You want him bangin' on the door? I won't have any problem tellin' him exactly what's goin' on."

"No!"

"Yep, now are you gonna behave?"

"Okay, okay."

"You asked for this," he declared, shifting her body and placing his leg over the back of hers.

"I did not!"

"Excuse me?"

"I told you I'd changed my mind."

"Now I'm gonna spank you real hard," he said sternly.

"What? Why?"

"You think you can pull that crap on me? You manipulated me into swattin' you 'cos you wanted to know how it felt, and I played along, but I'll only do that so much. The third time you cussed—that was how you told me to keep goin', and we both know it."

"I don't know anything of the sort!" she exclaimed, kicking out her feet.

"Damn, you are such a brat," he muttered, sliding her dress over her waist.

"No, Stop. What are you doing?"

Ignoring her protest, he stared down at her full, round rump encased in white lace, then pulling her panties into the cleft of her cheeks, he ran his palm over the bright pink flesh.

"Please," she begged, horrified her underwear had been so salaciously moved.

"You really like pushin' the envelope," he muttered. "No problem. I can push right back."

"No, no, honestly, I'm sorry."

"I think you've been messin' with guys your whole life," he remarked as he caressed and squeezed. "Well, little lady, you mess with me, you get your butt spanked."

"You're right, you're right," she said hastily, "but I won't mess with you anymore, I swear."

"Too late. Remember, no yellin'."

"No! Wait!"

But her feeble plea fell on deaf ears.

Lifting his hand he set to work in a steady pattern, landing his blows over the fullness of her cheeks before moving to the crease above her thighs.

"Ow, please, Beau, I'm sorry."

"I was just gonna give you a sexy little spankin'," he said, continuing to swat her backside. "You're the one who turned this into more."

"No, please stop, it hurts."

"Yep, this here's a proper spankin', what you've been askin' for since the day I met you. Tomorrow at the ranch you're gonna be polite and sweet, and no cussin', right?"

"Right," she panted, trying in vain to gyrate her hips away from his hot, slapping hand.

"It's important around my horses to do exactly what I say. Got it?"

"Yes, whatever you say, yes, yes."

"If you give me any of your sass you're goin' right back over my knee, and I won't be usin' my hand. Are we clear?"

"Ooh, Beau, yes, yes, we're clear. Please, stop."

"Now I'm gonna make sure," he said sternly, letting fly with a battery of rapid smacks that sent her howling into the mattress. "Okay, I'm done. I hope I've made my point."

"You have," she moaned, throwing back her hand to soothe the burn.

"Nope, you don't get to rub that butt until I say," he scolded, grabbing her wrist. "You stay as you are and feel that sting."

"It does sting," she bleated, squirming on his lap, "and it's hot."

But as she wriggled on his knees, his eye fell on the glistening dew between her legs.

"Nickie," he said softly, smoothing his palm across her seared crimson skin, "you really are a very naughty girl, but you're also very sexy." Slowly sliding his fingers between her legs, he slipped them into her drenched pussy. "How does this feel? Does it help?"

She stiffened for only a moment before letting out a heavy sigh.

"Ooh, yes, thank you."

"Well, whatta ya know, naughty Nickie said thank you. Manners like that will get you more."

Slipping his thumb against her clit, he circled and pressed, eliciting a deep, grateful moan, and as he pushed his index finger into her soaked channel, she spread her legs in what he assumed was an urgent request for more. He grit his teeth. His cock screamed for relief, but he hadn't brought a condom. No protection, no sex.

"Dammit. Well, there's more than one way."

Deftly pulling her up, he laid her over the edge of the bed and slid off her panties..

"God, Beau, I want you so much," she groaned staring at him over her shoulder.

"Let me see you rub that cute slitty," he said firmly, stripping off his slacks. "Do it right now, and arch your back and spread your legs."

As she dropped her head into the mattress, and darted her hand against her sex, he stood behind her, his cock in his hand.

"I'd love to slide into you right now, but it's gonna have to wait."

Slipping two fingers inside her sopping pussy, he thrust them in and out as he stroked himself, delighting in the sight of her reddened, wriggling backside.

"I'm so close," she suddenly exclaimed, bucking back against his hand. "God, I'm so close. Please don't stop."

Her unbridled excitement sent a rush of energy through his body, and as she buried her head in the mattress and let out a long, low wail, his climax abruptly threatened. Her pussy walls pulsed against his frigging fingers, fueling his imminent explosion, and with a guttural groan he erupted, his cream spilling over her chastised cheeks and dribbling down his hand.

Catching his breath he watched her fall limp on the bed, and with his heart still pounding, he moved into the bathroom, washed up, then returned to her with a damp hand towel. She had removed her dress and was lying on her stomach completely naked.

"Look at you."

"Please will you join me?"

"Sure, for a little while, then I've gotta head home," he murmured, gently wiping her clean.

Placing the facecloth on the nightstand, he pulled the covers over them and stretched out next to her.

"I didn't even get to meet these beautiful girls," he grinned, fondling her breasts.

"Ooh, don't stop," she begged, "please don't stop and please don't leave."

"I promise I'll give them plenty of attention next time, attention I'll bet they've never enjoyed before."

"Should they be worried?"

"That depends on you," he replied, lifting his gaze. "How's your butt?"

"Sore, thank you very much."

"You're very welcome."

"I didn't mean, thank you as in, thank you."

"Sure you did," he said softly.

Lowering his head, he gently kissed her, then wrapped her in his arms.

"Naughty Nickie, that's who you are, and I have a feelin' there'll be a lot more spankin' in your future."

"Not if I can help it."

"I know you have to say that," he said with a sigh, wishing he didn't need to leave, "but we both know I'm right."

A short time later, after a long, leisurely kiss goodbye at the door, Nicole padded back to her bed, laid down and stared at the ceiling. She'd imagined a sexy kiss and a small taste of spanking would be fun, but things had gone much further, and Beau had taken her breath away. She loved being called Naughty Nickie. She was falling for him—hard. Rolling on to her side she closed her eyes and inhaled the lingering scent of him on the pillow.

*If you give me any of your sass you're goin' right back over my knee, and I won't be usin' my hand, are we clear?*

His tantalizing threat danced through her mind. Moving her hand behind her, she touched her tender backside. She loved the hot, prickly sensation, and closing her eyes she tried to imagine what full-on sex would be like, but swept up by a yawn, she could feel sleep descending. Pulling the aromatic pillow close to her body, she began to drift away, but suddenly her life in the city cast a dark shadow.

"Gerald," she muttered. "Fuck. I have to deal with you, and I will, soon."

* * *

On the other side of town Beau was sitting on his back porch staring out at the horses in a nearby paddock. As he softly strummed his guitar a song began to reveal itself, the lyrics forming in his head as the melody evolved.

I don't know where you came from,
I don't know who you are,
I admit to feelin' kinda strange
And I'm likin' it so far,

You're a different kinda woman,
With a different kinda love,
A different kinda something

A naughty Angel from above.

Hurrying inside to make note of what he'd written, he scribbled the words, then let out a heavy sigh. He'd penned a number of songs, but none moved him in such a unique way.

Locking the door, he turned out the lights and ambled up the stairs to his bedroom, then stripping off, he strolled into his bathroom. Stepping into the shower to wash off the day, he wondered if he was on her mind as much as she was on his.

He grinned.

He'd left her with a sore backside.

He was on her mind whether she wanted him to be or not.

Turning off the faucets and toweling himself dry, he wandered into his bedroom, opened a small cabinet and retrieved a bottle of very old, very expensive scotch. Pouring himself a splash he downed it in one gulp, letting out a grunt as it hit his throat.

"Man, I needed that."

Resisting the urge to have another, he crawled into bed, and with the image of the sexy, spoiled young woman in the forefront of his mind, he closed his eyes and drifted into sleep.

# CHAPTER EIGHT

Stirred awake by the banging of his front door, Beau knew had to be Gina, and that meant he'd overslept. Stumbling to the window he spied his two ranch hands, Ben and Jeb, out in the paddocks with their wheelbarrows cleaning up the horse manure.

Yawning loudly, he padded into the bathroom and turned on the shower. In two short hours he'd be picking up Naughty Nickie and he couldn't wait. As he stepped under the hot water and dowsed his hair with shampoo, the image of her upturned bottom and bright red cheeks danced in his head bringing his cock to life. Leaning against the tiled wall he began to massage his rigid rod, thinking back to the delightful sounds she'd made as he'd spanked her, and the marvelous howl she'd let loose as she'd climaxed.

His mind jumped to the scene in the barn he'd envisioned earlier. He was seated on a bale of hay, her body across his lap, her bottom exposed and his slapping hand turning her skin beautifully pink, but the fantasy abruptly changed. She was kneeling in front of him, her mouth slurping his cock, her eyes gazing up at him adoringly.

The vision propelled him into his climax.

As it shuddered through his loins he groaned deeply, then let the hot stream blaze over him. A minute later, stepping out and toweling off, the song he'd started to write rang through his head.

I don't know where you came from,
I don't know who you are,
I admit to feelin' kinda strange
And I'm likin' it so far,

You're a different kinda woman,

With a different kinda love,
A different kinda something
A naughty Angel from above.

You're nowhere in sight,
But I can see you in my head,
I wanna wake up with you against me
I wanna see you in my bed.

You're a different kinda woman,
With a different kinda love,
A different kinda somethin'
A naughty Angel from above?

Wrapping a towel around his waist he hurried to the bureau against his window and quickly scribbled the new verse, making a mental note to take it downstairs and add to what was sitting on the notepad inside his desk drawer.  Glancing outside he saw Pepper, his handsome grey gelding, kicking up his heels and running around his paddock.

"I know how you feel buddy," he murmured. "I do too. Spooked, but happy, real happy."

Casting his eye further afield he smiled as he saw Trixie lying down basking in the morning sun. He laughed out loud.

"Trixie, you're nothin' like the girl who's gonna be sittin' on your back in a couple of hours, and it's just as well."

Dressing in his favorite riding jeans, a fresh white and blue checked cotton shirt and comfortable boots, he ran his fingers through his damp hair. He'd given up on the large shock that fell over his forehead. It had a mind of its own, and the girls at his local tavern told him it was sexy as hell. He wasn't sure if they were right, but he'd chosen to believe them. Trotting down the stairs he heard Gina busy at work in the kitchen, and as he neared he smelled the inviting aroma of freshly brewed coffee.

"Hey, Beau," she said with a welcoming smile. "Who's the lucky girl?"

Gina was in her 50's, but had one of those faces that didn't age, a figure that still turned heads, and a twinkle in her eye that Beau knew would never go out.

"Not what you'd expect," he replied pouring himself a mug of the tempting coffee.

"No? What do you think I'd expect," she quipped, flipping the bacon and cracking two eggs into the sizzling pan.

"She's from the city, wears makeup, she's got her own mind and not afraid to speak it. She's kinda..."

"Challenging?" Gina asked with a laugh.

"Well, yeah, I guess you could say that," Beau replied with a grin.

"I haven't seen that glint in your eye for a long time, if ever. I'm looking forward to meeting her. What's her name?"

"Nickie, uh, Nicole. No, Nickie."

"Which is it?"

"Her name's Nicole, but I call her Nickie," he replied, suddenly feeling flustered.

"Man, you've got it bad. How'd you meet her?"

"I don't have anything bad," he said hastily. "I'm gonna finish her house. She owns that half-built mess on the hill above the lake."

"You're not! It's an ugly monstrosity."

"Don't worry, Geoff's revamped the plans."

"Thank goodness," she replied plating his eggs and bacon. "Is she coming here so you can take her on one of your famous rides?"

"What do you mean, famous rides?"

"Just poking you," she giggled, "but are you? Going to take her for a ride I mean?"

"Yep, I'm gonna put her on Trixie. I thought we'd do the lake, then come back here for lunch, then, I dunno, maybe we'll cruise back up to the house and walk through the changes."

"Are you crazy?" she frowned placing the breakfast in front of him.

"What's crazy about that?" he asked dousing his food with pepper and hot sauce.

"If you want this to be a fun visit to a ranch don't take her to the biggest headache in her life. Have your lunch, then take her up to Flat Top Point and show her the amazing view."

"Gina, you're a genius! Huh. I like that. Gina the Genius. Why haven't I thought of that before?"

"I have no idea, but I'm glad you're finally noticing," she said with a sardonic lilt in her voice, then pausing, she added, "Something tells me I'd better change your sheets."

"Okay, this conversation has just crossed a line."

"Don't they always?" she said, winking as she wandered past him.

She disappeared from the room, and picking up his mug he smiled at the thought that she was right. He did indeed, need his sheets changed.

* * *

Nicole had slept late, and after enjoying a light breakfast through room service, she jumped under a hot shower. Unlike Beau, who had simply run his fingers through his wet hair and walked down the stairs, she spent almost thirty minutes styling. Her hairdryer and a round hairbrush created the desired result, but staring at her reflection she wasn't happy.

"I look too...too...what?"

As her reflection gazed back at her, the penny dropped.

"I look too much like Nicole and not enough like Nickie. I know exactly what to do."

Pulling off her robe, she turned the shower back on and let the water splash over her head, then stepping out she flicked on the hairdryer and let the hot air dry it without using her brush. It took longer than she thought it would, but when she was done her lips curled in a satisfied smile.

"There, that's better."

All the carefully styled waves were gone, and her hair was falling softly around her shoulders with a few wild flyaways.

Turning to her makeup tray, she decided against her usual red lipstick and dark mascara, opting for pink gloss and soft green eyeshadow, then wandered into the bedroom to dress.

At Wally's her eye had taken her to the red and white check shirt, but she decided to wear the more feminine pink and white instead. Humming happily she pulled off the tags and donned the clothes, and ambling back into the bathroom she grinned at her reflection.

"This is amazing. I look so much younger."

Glancing down at her watch, she discovered she had fifteen minutes before Beau was due to collect her. Returning to the room, she picked up the large tote she'd half-packed in the fervent hope she'd be spending the night. Inside was the aqua and white shirt, a fresh pair of panties and a pair of socks. Carrying it back into the bathroom, she threw in her lotions, makeup and a hairbrush.

"I'm forgetting something," she muttered, then suddenly remembered the gifts she'd bought. Moving back to the armoire and dropping them into the tote, she decided to wait for Beau in the lobby.

Heading out the door and down the hallway, she rode down in the elevator, stepped out and glanced through the large glass doors. The sun was glinting off the polished chrome of the parked cars. It promised to be a beautiful day. It was only a moment later the familiar turquoise truck rolled into the driveway.

Her butterflies sprang to life.

Moving slowly through the parking lot, it came to a stop under the portico. Nervously walking outside, she paused as he opened his door and climbed out. He looked even cuter in daylight than he had across the dinner table. She caught his eye, and breaking into a grin he hurried across the driveway to see her.

"You look amazin'," he exclaimed. "I can't believe it. I mean, you looked great before, but..."

"Thanks. I thought this was more what I needed to wear for your ranch."

"You were right."

Unexpectedly wrapping his arms around her, he hugged her tightly, then lifted her off her feet.

"What are you doing?"

"What I had to," he said with a chuckle as he stood her back on her feet. "You ready to sit on a horse?"

"Absolutely. Look, I even have the right boots."

"I see that. Good old Wally. He'll never steer you wrong."

Taking her tote, he put his arm around her shoulder and walked her to the truck.

"Nickie?" he murmured, opening the door.

"Yes?"

"Your butt's not too sore to ride, is it?"

"Seriously?" she retorted, feeling her face blush.

"It's a simple question."

"Get in the car and start driving, cowboy."

Beau laughed out loud as he closed her door, then trotted around to get in behind the wheel.

"Care to share the joke," she asked as he grinned across at her.

"I'm just lookin' forward to the day."

"Yeah? Me too."

## CHAPTER NINE

Beau's ranch was further from the hotel than Nickie had imagined, and the house and barn were set at the end of a long, gravel driveway flanked on either side by white fenced paddocks. As they rolled to a stop she saw two horses at a hitching post saddled up, standing completely relaxed with their eyes half-closed. One was grey, the other brown and white.

"I'm so excited," she exclaimed. "Which one is Trixie?"

"Trixie's the paint."

"The paint?"

"The one that's not grey," he said with a grin.

"That makes sense. I can see why a horse with those patchy colors would be called a paint horse. Cool. Can I go over there?"

"You don't wanna drop your bag inside first?"

"Hardly. I've never even touched a horse and I'm dying to do this."

Her enthusiasm bubbled over, her face lighting up like a little girl on Christmas morning.

"Then let's go. I'll introduce you."

As they climbed from the truck and started forward, both Pepper and Trixie pricked up their ears and turned to look at them.

"Oh, my gosh, I can't believe this," she said with giggle. "Thank you so much for bringing me here."

He stared down at her glowing smile. The bitchy, demanding female he'd first met had transformed into a bright, cheerful young woman.

"You're welcome. I'm really glad this is making you so happy."

"Wow," she breathed as they reached Trixie's side. "She's so beautiful."

"You can pet her, just run your hand down her neck."

"She's so soft. Beau, I feel all...weird."

"Weird, how?"

"You'll think I'm an idiot."

"I doubt that."

"I felt—I feel—this thing," she breathed moving closer to the horse and continuing to stroke her. "An emotional thing. It's crazy."

As she lifted her eyes, he could see it. They sparkled up at him, appearing almost teary.

"I have no idea why this is happening. I just feel kind of—joyous."

"Horses have unique energy. It's blowin' me away that you're gettin' that. You wanna get on board?"

"Really? Right now?"

"Sure, unless you don't feel like you're ready, or sittin' on a saddle might be a bit uncomfortable," he quipped with a wink.

"Stop it! I'm totally ready, yes, definitely. I'm just so excited I can hardly stand it."

"Stay there for a minute, I'm gonna get you a helmet."

She watched him disappear into the barn, then leaning forward she began talking to Trixie in a soft, sweet voice.

"You are so beautiful. I don't know why I haven't done this before. Of course in the city it wouldn't be like this. I wouldn't be surrounded by all the trees and the quiet."

"Try this," Beau said, reappearing with a helmet.

"It's not very, uh, it looks kind of dorky. Are you sure I need it? I mean, we'll only be walking, right? What can happen if we're walking?"

"This thing is goin' on your head or you're not gettin' on the horse."

"Fine," she said, taking it from his hands and pushing it down on her head. "I'm so happy right now I don't really care."

"Nickie, that looks really good on you. I just need to close the strap under your chin."

Moving closer and taking hold of the plastic snaps, his eyes fell on her lips. The pink moistness beckoned him, and leaning in, he softly touched his mouth to hers.

A bolt of sexual energy surged through her body. Her butterflies began to flutter, and pressing her body against him, she moved her arms around his neck. His cock was suddenly hard against her, and when he broke the kiss, she let out a soft sigh and smiled up at him.

"Are you pleased to see me or is that a cellphone in your pocket?"

"Damn, girl, we'd better get you on that horse before we end up on a heap of straw in that barn."

"What if, I were to, uh..."

"What?"

"What if I were to say, fuck, let's do it."

"Those are fightin' words, missy," he said with a chuckle. "That might've worked last night, but next time you provoke me you might not like the response quite so much."

The fluttering butterflies exploded into a frenzy.

"Um, I'm not sure what to say to that."

"I think it's time I walked Trixie to the mounting block."

Taking a breath, she watched him step away and lift the reins looped over the hitching post.

"Come on," he said with a wink, leading the mare across the yard.

Shaking herself out of her minor stupor, she strode briskly to catch up.

"I'm guessing I get on top of this thing?" she remarked, standing by the steps of the mounting block.

"Yep. I've adjusted the stirrups. I think they should be about right. Put your foot in, swing your leg over, and sit down gently."

"I'm so nervous. She won't move or anything, right?"

"Nope, she's on tranquilizers and I'm holdin' her."

"Really? You've doped her?"

"Good lord, no, I was just kiddin'. She's super mellow."

"Why didn't you just say that?"

"Nickie, get on," he said firmly, shaking his head.

Gripping the saddle horn, she put her foot in the stirrup, and hoisted herself into place.

"That was so easy. Wow, it's cool up here. I like it a lot."

"Good, now just hold the reins like this," he explained taking her fingers and placing them around the leather straps. "It's just like you've probably heard. If you want to turn right, pull right, left, pull left. To stop, just give a gentle tug backwards with both reins and say ho. I'm gonna lead you back over to Pepper, that's my horse. All we'll be doin' is walkin', and Trixie will be glued to Pepper's side. You won't have to worry about steerin', but you should know at least that little bit."

"Beau, I'm loving every second," she said gratefully, leaning forward and patting Trixie's neck, "and she's such a sweet horse."

"Okay, I'm gonna lead her now. Sit up straight and relax."

As Beau began moving slowly away from the mounting block, Nickie felt confident enough to lift her eyes and take in her surroundings. Beau's house was a two-story chalet style A-Frame, and looked like something she'd seen in travelogues advertising the mountains in Switzerland.

"Your home is gorgeous," she sighed. "It looks like it belongs here, surrounded by all the pine trees and paddocks."

"Thanks, but look where you're goin'. When you're on a horse you always wanna have your eyes ahead. Hold on to this for a second."

"Okay," she murmured, smiling happily and taking the rope with which he'd been leading her. "This is so much fun."

Lifting Pepper's reins from the post, Beau swung himself into the saddle, then shifting his horse next to Trixie, he reached across and took back the lead rope.

"You've got your reins if you need them, but leave them loose for the moment. I'll be leadin' you along until you feel comfortable."

"Like training wheels."

"Yep, like trainin' wheels. You ready?"

"I am, but I think I can manage without you taking me. I feel really good."

"Just for a little while, but you look good up there."

"I feel amazing," she exclaimed. "In fact, I think this is one of the best times I've ever had."

* * *

The trail Beau had chosen skirted the lake, but he planned to break off at the midway point, travel up a gentle slope, and catch another trail on the other side that would drop them back on to his property. They'd only been riding a short time before the lake came into view, and feeling completely comfortable, Nicke didn't see the need for Beau to continue to lead her.

"It's your first time on a horse, and you might think you're ready, but you're not."

"But I'm fine. I'm holding the reins, see?"

Pulling Pepper to a halt he pointed to the lake.

"Instead of arguin', take a minute and look at what you're missin'."

Shifting her gaze, she stared out at the view and broke into a smile.

"You're right, it's gorgeous."

"I'll give up this lead rope when I think it's time. Keep complainin' and I'll take you outta that saddle and spank you again."

"So we disagree about things, you'll threaten to spank me?"

"Yep, that's about the size of it," he replied with a nod, and giving Pepper a gentle squeeze, he moved forward.

But there was a very good reason Beau needed to keep control of Trixie.

The trail was designated for horses, but a group of rebellious teenage boys had been seen racing their bicycles at breakneck speed.

"Nickie, tell me about your job. Won't you have to be headin' home soon?"

"I don't want to talk about that," she said briskly. "I'm here to get away from it."

"You don't have to take my head off. It was just a simple question."

"Sorry Beau. It's just not something I want to discuss, at least, not now."

"No problem. We don't have to talk at all. We can just enjoy the serenity of this place, and horses have a way of makin' you feel better no matter what the problem is."

Shifting her gaze back to the lake, she shook off the irritation, then patted Trixie's neck.

"You're right. They have such wonderful energy."

"They do," he said solemnly. "Horses have helped me through some real tough times."

"Beau, I'm going to learn how to ride and I'm buying a horse!" she suddenly exclaimed.

"Where are you going to learn, and where are you going to keep it?"

"You can teach me and I can keep it at your ranch. I'll pay you of course."

Beau stared at her for a minute, then began laughing so hard he had to pull up.

"Why is that funny?" she demanded. "Stop laughing at me!"

"It's how you say things," he replied, finally able to compose himself. "Don't get me wrong. A horse would be great for you, hell, a horse is great for anyone."

"Then why was it funny?"

"Nickie, I've never met anyone like you. I'm going to teach you how to ride! That's it, Nickie has spoken. Did it ever occur to you to ask me if I'd like to teach you how to ride?"

"Why would I? You'd like to, right?"

"That's hardly the point."

But the confounded look on her face sent him laughing again, and it was unexpectedly contagious.

"Beau! The fact that you'd like to teach me is blatantly obvious. How is that amusing? Now I'm laughing and I don't even know why."

"You are precious. Come here, I need to kiss you."

Leaning across, he grabbed the back of her neck and dropped his lips lightly on hers.

"You're right, I'd love to teach you," he said, pulling away, "but not just about horses."

"Cool."

"I'm not sure how long you'll think that, especially when your butt's on fire."

Goosebumps had popped from his soft kiss, and now his comment sent a hot flush across her face.

"We'd better get movin' or we'll be out here all day," he murmured, "and Gina's cooked us lunch."

"Who's Gina?"

"She's my housekeeper, cook, laundry person, whatever needs doin'," he replied as they started off.

"Oh, so she's your maid."

"No, I wouldn't call her my maid, she's more like a...hold up!"

"What is it?"

"Dammit. You hear that?"

"Kids yelling?"

"Yep, and they're gonna come around that corner on mini-bikes. It might upset the horses," he said urgently. "Sit up, and if Trixie starts jiggin' don't pull on the reins, I've got her. Grab her mane or the saddle horn. Reins aren't for balance. Got it?"

"Shit! Yeah, I've got it," she replied feeling a ripple of fear shiver down her spine.

"You'll be fine," he promised, moving Pepper closer to Trixie.

Beau had been staying alert, but it was the prick of Pepper's ears that told him something was ahead, and seconds later he'd heard the kids himself. Though confident his horses would probably be okay, a young woman had recently been circled by the wayward youths, terrifying both her and her mare. Alone he'd have had no qualms jumping off and nabbing them, but he couldn't put Nickie at risk.

"Okay, here they come," he warned, hearing their approach. "Remember, sit up and stay calm. Trixie can't go anywhere, I've got her."

"Fuck. Sorry, but fuck!"

The teens suddenly appeared in the distance riding their small bikes at breakneck speed, but seeing Beau and Nickie, they stood up, whooping in an obvious effort to scare the horses.

Pepper began to react.

Beau stroked his neck to settle him. A few seconds later Trixie became agitated, but Beau knew Trixie was reacting to Pepper, not the bikers.

"Fuck, fuck," Nickie whispered as the kids sped toward her.

"You're all right, stay calm," Beau said steadily. "They'll be past us real quick."

Beau was right, but they screamed and waved their hands as they whizzed by, causing both horses to dance in fright.

"Damn," he growled as he settled Pepper. "I'm gonna find those boys! How you doin', Nickie? You okay?"

"Not really, kind of, I guess so."

"You did good," he said softly, reaching out and rubbing her arm. "Real good, and Trixie was a star. Try to relax."

"Who are those bastards?"

"I'm gonna call Tyler," he said, reaching for his phone. "He's a buddy of mine and a cop. Maybe he can get here in time to catch 'em."

As he placed the call, Nickie continued stroking Trixie's neck and telling her what a wonderful horse she was. When he finished talking, he smiled across at her.

"That calmed you both down."

"It know," she said with a sigh. "I love horses and I didn't even know it."

"Aren't you glad I insisted on keepin' this lead rope now?"

"Yes, but you could have told me we might run into those brats."

"What for? You'd have done nothin' but worry."

"Oh, yeah, I guess you're right."

"Let's move on. We'll be ridin' up a hill in a minute or two, and once we're headin' towards home, you can take the reins. Trixie will know where she's goin'. You won't even have to steer."

"Cool."

"Again with the cool?"

"Uh-huh."

A few minutes later they started to climb the gentle slope, and halfway up, she glanced down at the lake below.

"Beau, this is gorgeous."

"After lunch I'm gonna drive you to Flat Top Point. It's above the ranch. You can see forever."

"I'd like to see forever."

"It's a truly amazin' view. Okay, we'll be headin' down in a minute. Remember what I said, look ahead."

As they crested the top of the hill and she saw his ranch, she felt a swell of emotion. She loved the trees, the clean air, the mirror lake, and especially the horses.

And then there was Beau.

# CHAPTER TEN

Following the trail back to the ranch, avoiding conversation about Nickie's life in the city, Beau chatted about his horses and their different personalities. As she asked endless questions, it became clear she was fascinated with all things equine.

"What do they eat?" she said enthusiastically as they rode into the stable area and came to a stop. "Besides grass and hay obviously."

"Saddles off first," he said patiently, delighted by her interest, "then we'll brush them off and take them back to their paddocks."

Jumping off Pepper, he looped the reins around the hitching post and turned to help her dismount, but she was already sliding from the saddle. Quickly placing his hands around her waist, he guided her down.

"Thanks," she said shifting around to face him.

"I'm glad you had such a good time."

"I absolutely loved it, except for those kids, but even then..."

Her eyes twinkled up at him, and as she moved her body against his and brought her arms around his neck, he felt his pulse quicken and his sleeping cock stir in his jeans.

"We've gotta take care of the horses."

"Can't you give a girl a quick kiss?"

"Yep, but I'm not sure I can quit there."

"Works for me," she murmured with a sassy grin.

Wrapping her in his arms, he planted his mouth on hers, and as the kiss grew fervent, he wanted to whisk her into the barn and rip off her clothes.

"We've gotta take care of the horses," he repeated as he pulled back.

"Right now?"

"Yep, right now, but it won't take long. I'll show you how to get this saddle off."

Willing his cock to calm down, he stepped around her, unbuckled the saddle and lifted it off the mare's back.

"Here," he said, offering it to her.

"Sure," she muttered, taking it from his hands. "Good grief. This thing's heavy."

"Carry it into the barn, I'll be right behind you. You'll see an empty saddle rack next to the others."

"This is worse than doing weights in a gym," she grunted as she started forward.

Watching to make sure she got safely through the door, he removed his saddle from Pepper, then followed her inside. She was standing in front of the saddles and bridles, her back to him with her hands on her hips. Her curvaceous backside seemed to be begging for attention. He glanced at his watch. The boys would be at lunch. Darting forward, he grabbed her elbow, hustled her to a nearby bale of hay, and dropping down, he yanked her across his lap.

"Beau! What the hell?"

"I'm just gonna give you a quick spankin'," he declared dispatching his hand with a sound swat.

"Ow! Why?"

"Because, Nickie, you need it," he exclaimed, raining slaps on her upturned behind. "You're gonna ask nicely for things in future, not demand or expect them."

"Ow, ow. Okay, you've made your point!"

"A few more, real hard, then we'll be done for now!"

"For now? You've got to be—!"

"No more talkin'," he declared, continuing to land his hot slaps. "Be still and take your spankin'."

"Ooh, Beau," she protested, squirming as she spoke.

"What did I just say?"

"Sorry," she wailed, his palm landing a volley of fiery swats.

"We're done, and next time do as you're told," he scolded, helping her to her feet.

"Did you have to do that?"

"If you meant what you said and you wanna learn from me, you can expect more quick spankin's just like that one," he said softly, wrapping his arms around her, "but if you've changed your mind, no problem."

"I don't know what to say, except..."

"Except?" he crooned, moving his lips to her neck.

"Except—I want to be naked with you, and I swear, what you just did made me want you even more."

"Feelin's mutual," he purred, sucking in her skin, "but first we've gotta brush off our horses and take them to their paddocks."

"You're not making it easy."

"Back at ya," he said with a grin as he released her. "Follow me, I'll show you how to pick out Trixie's feet."

Moving to a nearby tack trunk, he retrieved a plastic tack box filled with grooming supplies.

"Pick out her feet?" she repeated, her backside on fire, and aching to curl up against his chest.

"Yep. The faster we get this done, the faster we can get in the house and have lunch."

"Lunch? Who gives a fuck about lunch?"

"Excuse me?"

"Sorry, sorry, who cares about lunch. Is that better?"

"Yep, and if I hadn't just spanked you, I'd be doin' it right now. You're too pretty to have a mouth like that. Now follow me," he said sternly, trying to ignore his bursting cock as he walked outside to the horses. "Stand there and watch, I'll show you how this is done."

Taking a deep breath and resisting the temptation to sidle up to him to steal another kiss, she stood quietly as he lifted Trixie's foot and scraped out the dirt she'd picked up on the trail.

"Now you do the other one," he said, straightening up and handing her the hoof pick.

They continued grooming the horses, but she found it difficult to focus. Every time she looked at him she'd notice the long black lashes framing his crystal blue eyes, his much-too-kissable lips, and his wide shoulders and muscled arms.

"Are you okay?" he asked, as they started leading the horses to their paddocks. "You're suddenly very quiet."

"It's either that or speak my mind."

"Speakin' your mind is preferable."

"But I say things you don't like."

"Only cussin'. Please tell me what's on your mind. Are you upset because I put you over my knee again?"

"Uh, no."

"Then tell me what's botherin' you."

"Fine! I bet every girl in town is after you."

"Nickie! Why would you say something like that?"

"Even that kid, Amy, at the hotel, even she wants you."

"Nickie, you're a gorgeous, sexy woman, and I could say the same. You must have a dozen guys bangin' at your door back in the city."

"The men I've known, the men I know," she said with a heavy sigh, "they're all so predictable."

"Nickie, what you said about the men you know. They're predictable."

"Yeah?"

"Predictable is another word for borin', right?"

"Yeah, I guess it is."

"Don't get me wrong, there are some real fine ladies around here, but they're kinda like those guys. More importantly, there's a thing called chemistry. You ever heard of that?"

"Of course," she replied, a slight grin curling her lips.

"I kinda think that might be happenin' here."

"Um, I think you might be right."

They'd reached the fields, and leading Pepper into his paddock, Beau returned to Nickie and they continued the short distance to the next gate. Walking in with her, he stood at her side as she undid Trixie's halter and set her free.

"You've had your first ride, cleaned up your horse and brought her back to her paddock. How do you feel?"

"It's fantastic, Beau, and I want to do it all again, all of it. Thank you so much."

"I'm glad. I truly am. Now we can kick back."

"Beau, when we get to the house," she murmured, "can lunch

wait?"

His cock coming back to life, he stared down at her.

"Nickie, lunch can wait for a month of Sundays."

* * *

The moment they walked through the door Beau swept her into his arms, carried her up the stairs to his bedroom and laid her on the bed.

"Do exactly as I say," he murmured, sitting on the edge of the bed. "Can you manage that?"

"Uh-huh."

"Close your eyes. I'll tell you when you can open them."

"Beau, you're turning me on so much."

"Back at ya, sweetheart."

As she squeezed her eyes shut, he began unbuttoning her blouse, taking his time as he relished her soft moans. Moving back the folds of fabric, he found her voluptuous breasts encased in a lacy pink bra. Pausing a moment to soak in the sight, he lowered his head to kiss his way across her cleavage, then sent his lips to nuzzle her neck.

"That feels so good," she mumbled, bringing her arms around him.

"Not yet, sugar," he purred, gently pulling them away.

Rising up, he moved to the foot of the bed to unlace her paddock boots. Wriggling them off and finding pink socks, he grinned as he wondered if her panties would match, then stretching across her body, he unsnapped the button at the waistband of her jeans and slid down the zipper.

Pink lace.

His smile grew wider.

"Aren't you just a picture," he murmured, sliding the denim pants down her legs and tossing them aside.

Quickly stripping, he stretched out beside her, removed her blouse and unsnapped her bra, then roamed his hands over her luscious breasts.

"It's gonna be real hard to ever leave this bed," he crooned, his lips and tongue exploring her neck and chest.

"Beau, please, please," she whimpered. "I want you so much."

Moving his fingers between her legs and trailing them against the gusset of her panties, he let out a low whistle.

"You're soaked, and just for me. What's gonna happen when I slip my fingers inside?"

"Do it," she muttered frantically, lifting her hand and attempting to push down the lacy underwear.

"Naughty Nickie," he scolded. "Get that hand outta the way."

"Beau, please touch me. I need you to."

"Do as I say and I will, but if you don't—"

Before he could finish, she yanked her arm down.

"Good girl, you're learnin," he said, giving her a quick kiss, then sliding the panties down her legs, he slipped his fingers into her pussy.

"Damn, girl, you're really wet."

"I want you, I do, I really want you."

"You can open your eyes," he whispered, his lips at her ear. "Now spread, sugar, spread your legs real wide for me," he continued, locking her gaze as she stared up at him. "Yeah, like that. You need to show me just how much you want my cock before I'll let you have it."

"I do, I swear."

"I'm startin' to believe you," he replied, lapping at her neck, then tonguing his way to her nipples. "Lay back and close your eyes again."

"Beau, I love how you're controlling me."

"I know what you need."

Closing his lips around the perfect, pink cherry tip, he sucked and nibbled, then thrust two fingers inside her soaked sex.

"You're making me crazy," she moaned, wriggling against his hand. "Really crazy."

"We can't have that," he drawled, lifting his head. "Time to move on your stomach," he declared, rolling her over. "Look at that lovely red ass. It should always be red, red and hot."

Moving his palm across her cheeks, he landed a quick slap, knowing it wouldn't take much to fire up a tantalizing sting. She yelped, and he smacked her again, then pushing her legs apart, he knelt between them, grabbed her hips and pulled them up.

"You want my cock?"

"Yes, yes, yes, take me," she panted, pushing herself up on her hands and wriggling her backside at him. "Take me right now!"

"That sounded like an order," he said sternly, the head of his cock teasing her portal. "I don't take orders, I give 'em. You ask real polite and sweet, I might think about it.

"Please, Beau, please make love to me. I'll be good, I swear."

"That was close. Try again."

"What do you want me to say?" she begged, her voice a desperate groan.

"You asked me, but I didn't hear you wantin' or needin' my cock."

"Ooh, this is torture."

"I can always stop."

"No! Please, Beau, I've never felt like this before, not ever. I want you so much, I need you inside me, please?"

"There you go. Drop on your elbows, arch your back, and stick your ass out."

As she lowered herself back down, he leaned across the bed, pulled open the drawer of his nightstand and grabbed a condom. Her gasping breaths matched his own hot desire, and hurriedly sliding on the protection, he placed himself at her entrance and pushed forward.

Her grateful cry bounced off the walls, and as he began to thrust, relishing the feel of her and the glorious sight of her spanked ass, her squeals grew louder and more frequent. He accelerated, pumping harder and gripping her waist.

"You're so strong," she suddenly exclaimed. "So strong and so big."

Plunging forward with a quick, strong stroke, he followed it by another, and another, continuing without pause as he moved his fingers beneath her pelvis and sought out her clit.

"If you do that—"

"If I do this, what?" he teased, urgently rubbing the magic nub.

"I'm already s-so close—your c-cock..." she stammered. "Ooh, Beau..."

"I'm gonna ride you hard," he warned, shifting his hand back to grasp her hip. "If you wanna put your fingers on your clit, you go ahead, but you'd better not come before I say you can."

Shifting slightly on his knees and holding her tightly, he pitched forward and began pummeling her pussy. Energy surged through his loins, and he knew he couldn't hold back another second.

"Come now," he commanded, landing a solid slap, "right now!"

She wailed as her explosion took hold, sending him over the edge. Intense tingles permeated his being, his fingers dug into her flesh, and as he listened to her shudder through the orgasmic spasms, his own convulsions rippled through his limbs.

But the moment abruptly passed, and slipping out of her, utterly drained, he collapsed on the bed.

## CHAPTER ELEVEN

Slipping into the shower and soaping off each other's bodies, Nickie realized she'd left her bag in his truck. Drying off and dressing, Beau left to retrieve it. Stepping from the stall and rubbing a towel across her wet skin, she donned his black, terry cloth robe, and stared at her reflection in the bathroom mirror.

"This is a hell of a pickle you've got yourself into, Nicole Harris," she muttered, but hearing him on the stairs, she let out a troubled sigh and walked into the bedroom.

"Here you go," Beau declared, placing the bag on the bed. "I'm gonna warm up our lunch."

Tilting his head he paused for a moment, then abruptly strode across the room and hugged her tightly.

"You look real good in my robe."

"It feels real good, and it smells like you."

"Is that a good thing?"

"Of course," she said with a laugh.

"You wear it any time you want. I'll see you in the kitchen, then we'll go for that drive."

"Perfect. Uh, Beau?"

"You need somethin'?" he asked breaking their hug.

"No, just, that was heavenly, and I think you're wonderful."

"Back at ya," he replied with a wink.

Pushing back a wave of emotion as she watched him leave, she opened her bag and pulled out her fresh shirt and jeans.

"Maybe I should tell him," she muttered, "or would that just fuck everything up?"

* * *

A short time later, as Beau stared at Nickie across the table, he felt something akin to joy; it was the only word he could think of to describe the energy pulsing in his heart. He'd been in lust, he'd been in crush, he'd even thought he'd been in love a couple of times, but this was a high he'd not experienced.

"Why are you looking at me like that?" she asked drinking the last of her tea.

"The aqua in that shirt brings out the green of your eyes, and you look peaceful."

"That ride, and I mean the one on Trixie," she added with a giggle, "then, uh, being with you, that's enough to calm down anyone, even me."

"This tranquil Nickie suits you. The perfect frame of mind for where we're goin'. Are you ready to take a ride?"

"I'm not sure."

"Your butt too sore?"

"Why do you ask me questions like that?" she retorted, her eyes wide.

"Cos it gets that reaction," he replied with a chuckle. "I wasn't talkin' about a horse ride, I was talkin' about gettin' in the jeep and drivin' up to Flat Top Point. Thought maybe we could take dessert with us, and a bottle of wine if you'd like. If we stay long enough, we can watch the sunset."

"That sounds fabulous. Does your maid come back tonight?"

"Gina isn't my maid."

"She cooks, she cleans, she does housework and you pay her, right?"

"Yeah, but—"

"Then she's your maid."

"Technically, maybe, but I don't see her that way. Gina's one of my best friends."

"You can't be friends with the people who work for you. My dad always said that."

"In this case he's wrong. Help me clear the table and we can take off."

Though tempted to debate the point, she picked up some plates and carried them to the counter.

"Beau, I love your house. It's so warm. It says, come in and put your feet up."

"Thanks. That's what a house should say."

"Mine doesn't, or rather won't when it's done. I thought I wanted something super modern."

"Are you changin' your mind?"

"I think I am. I want something cozy like this."

"What you're suggestin' isn't a big deal. It just means puttin' up some walls, and Nickie, I'm happy you're thinkin' that way."

"All I've ever known is architectural. That's what everyone has at home. A home like this never occurred to me. I want a sloped roof too, and paned windows, and—"

"Whoa, this is all great, but if you're gonna make that many changes we need a meetin' with Geoff."

"You're going to build my house, aren't you, Beau?" she murmured, walking up and pecking him on the cheek.

"Looks like it, and now you're talkin' about a house I wanna build. You're talkin' about a home."

"That's it exactly, I want to build a home."

He took the dishes from her and placed them in the sink, then wiped his hands on a towel and wrapped her into an engulfing hug.

"You're like that diamond in the rough, sharp edges and tough as nails, but underneath you're waiting to sparkle."

"Beau…that's the nicest thing anyone's ever said to me."

"I mean it," he murmured. "Let's get things cleaned up. I really wanna show you this view."

"And I really want to see it, but, um, Beau, before we do that, I have something for you. A thank you. It's not a big deal, just a couple of things I picked up at Wally's."

"You're kiddin'?"

"No, I'll be right back," she said happily, and breaking from his hug she hurried towards the stairs.

He finished cleaning up, then retrieved the picnic basket from the hall closet. As he began packing the wine and a variety of delicious treats, he couldn't help thinking how unique Nickie had turned out to be.

"I almost changed my mind about one of these," she announced as she walked back in.

"Because?"

"You'll see," she replied offering him a Wally's shopping bag filled with tissue.

"I can't believe you did this," he stammered, taking it from her. "Thank you."

Placing the bag on the table, he dropped his hand inside, only to find a riding crop with a large leather tongue in the shape of a heart.

"Ah, I see," he muttered with a wide grin. "This what you almost changed your mind about?"

"Uh-huh."

"I have a feelin' it's gonna come in real handy," he remarked, swishing it through the air.

"I'm such an idiot!"

"I think you're a genius," he said with a chuckle.

"Okay, okay, keep looking."

Laying the crop on the table, he peered into the bag and spied a highly polished, small wooden box. Pulling it out he recognized the famous label, and lifting the lid he gazed down at a stainless steel pocketknife, the handle artfully inlaid with mother-of-pearl.

"I figured, being both a cowboy and a contractor, a tool like that might be handy."

"Nickie, you didn't have to do this."

"I didn't do it because I had to, I did it because I wanted to. Do you like it?"

"Are you kiddin'? I love it! I've always wanted one of these. Thank you. What happened to that crazy woman I met?"

"I guess you're a good influence."

"Come here," he said with a sigh, opening his arms.

As she sank against his chest, he could hardly believe she was the same rude, obnoxious female that had been so demanding and difficult. He decided she must have been a very frustrated and angry young woman.

* * *

A short time later they were in the jeep, the picnic basket filled with goodies and a bottle of Merlot, sitting on the back seat. Driving up a dirt road, though it wasn't steep, the view was becoming spectacular.

"There's a huge flat pad up ahead," Beau declared. "I'm plannin' on buildin' a cabin up here one of these days. A place to escape to when I need it."

"A romantic getaway?" Nickie asked.

"I like the sound of that."

They continued to climb, and as the jeep crested the gentle slope, she was amazed by the size of the flat pad appearing before her.

"This is weird! It's like someone cut off the top of the hill. Did you grade this?"

"Nope, nature did. I call it Flat Top Point. We get bad winds a few times a year, and up here, whoa, it can blow you right over. That's the only problem. Check out the trees over there?"

Staring across to a thicket in the distance, she could see some of the trees appeared to be leaning backwards, and others to the side.

"That looks really strange, but you know when the winds are coming, right?"

"Yep. They kick up at the beginnin' of summer, right about now. They'll be hittin' soon. I never come here when it's windy."

"It's that bad?"

"It's that bad," he said grimly, "and I can't imagine you'd ever do this, but don't think about comin' up here to check it out for yourself," he warned. "That would be a really bad idea."

"Of course I wouldn't," she gaped at him. "That's crazy."

"Just wanna be clear, but look, we're almost at the spot," he said pointing ahead. "See the lake?"

The vastness of the still water came into view, and the hills on the opposite side seemed to fall directly into it.

"It's like a fiord. Wow. Absolutely stunning."

Pulling the jeep to a stop, they climbed out, and he grabbed the basket from the back seat.

"I've never seen anything like this," she murmured. "You own this hill?"

"Yep. Well, me and the bank," he said with a grin, "but not for much longer."

"Thank you so much for bringing me up here. Look, you can see the trail we were on."

"You can see everything from up here," he remarked, pulling a cheesecake and the bottle of wine from the hamper.

Dropping on to the soft, grassy ground, she pulled her knees into her chest and hugged them as she took in the remarkable view. She felt far away from her old life, but she knew it was a mirage. She was still in her old life, and it was a big problem.

"Here," he said, offering her a glass of wine.

"Perfect. Thanks."

"Anything you wanna talk about?" .

"Is it that obvious?"

"Kinda."

Sipping her wine, she moved her eyes from the view and stared up at the sky.

"I feel like I could reach up and touch the clouds," she murmured, "and this wine is really good."

Not wanting to push, he picked up a spoon, scooped up a large piece of the rich dessert, and brought it to her lips. Opening her mouth, she took in the entire bite.

"Mmmm, amazing. Who made this?"

"The maid," he replied sarcastically.

"Holy crap. She could be a chef. That's the best dessert I've ever had."

"Besides cheesecake, what's your favorite thing to eat?"

"I like food with bold flavors. Really good Indian food, or Thai is great too. Your turn."

As the sun continued its journey across the sky, they shared, laughed and debated. When they'd finished off the wine and devoured every last crumb of the cheesecake, he took the empty wine glass from her hand and placed it carefully to the side.

"One of these days," he purred, pushing her on her back and

straddling her lap, "I'm gonna take you into that thicket of trees, and do some really wicked things to you."

"Like what?"

"I'll bring up some rope," he murmured, pinning her wrists on either side of her head, "that riding crop you bought me, and make your hair stand on end. I don't mean the hair on your head."

"Do you have either of those things in the car?" she breathed, a flood of longing washing through her sex.

"You're even naughtier than I thought. Tonight, if you'd like to stay, I might give you an appetizer, but it might be too much for you."

"You won't know unless you try."

Smiling devilishly, he lowered his mouth to the base of her neck, trailed his tongue to her lips, and pushed it between her teeth. As their tongues danced, he lowered himself on top of her.

"I wanna devour you," he growled, pulling back and locking her eyes.

"And I want you to!"

"You are refreshingly honest. Sometimes it's not so good, but other times, like this..."

"I'm not sure what you mean."

"Most girls, they like to play it cool, not show their feelin's, but with you, I know what's goin' on with you every minute."

Before she could respond, he kissed her again, a burning possession of her mouth that made him want to rip her clothes off and ravage her, but as they broke apart, he sensed her worry had returned.

"Like now," he said softly, moving off her body and helping her sit up. "Whatever was buggin' you earlier is back. Can you tell me what it is?"

"It's not that I don't want to," she said softly, staring down at the trail they'd ridden, "it's just—Beau!" she suddenly exclaimed. "Look down there."

Following her line of sight, he saw a group of mini-cyclists having a party.

"I'm callin' Tyler. He might be able to nail those jerks," he declared, and jumping to his feet, raced to the car.

* * *

Watching him jog back to the jeep, she rolled her eyes. She'd been a hair's breath from telling him the dark secret. Staring back at the lake, she wondered if she should just take care of the mess by herself and leave him out of it. Was there anything to be gained by telling him?

* * *

Fifteen minutes later, as Nickie continued to ponder the state of her life, and Beau watched the police round up the teenagers and place them in handcuffs, a black Mercedes 65SL cruised off the interstate highway and glided through the winding road towards Lake Shimwah. Behind the wheel, a dark-haired somber man checked his navigator. Thirty-minutes and he'd be knocking on Nickie's hotel door.

## CHAPTER TWELVE

A short while after returning from their hilltop picnic, Tyler stopped by with good news. Over coffee and cake he told them the troublemaking teens had been caught smoking marijuana and drinking beer.

"Really glad we finally nailed them," Tyler declared, rising from the table. "I wish I could stay, but I have to get back to the station. Good to meet you, Nickie. I'm sure our paths will cross again."

"I hope so."

Waving him off, Beau put his arm around her and walked her back inside.

"Ready for an early night?" he asked, his voice husky as he pulled her against his body.

"Are you asking me to stay?"

"Yep."

"I'd love it."

Locking the door and turning out the lights, he led her up the stairs and into his room. Turning on only a small lamp on the nightstand, he gripped her arms and turned her to face him.

"I'm goin' into my closet, and when I get back, I wanna find you naked and in bed. Say, yes, Sir."

A thrill rippled through her body.

"Yes, Sir."

"Good girl," he growled, clutching her hair and jerking back her head. "I won't be long."

Devouring her mouth with a crushing, fervent kiss, he abruptly released her, then strode across the room and disappeared through a door against the far wall.

Heart racing, and her breath coming in quick gasps, she hurriedly undressed, and was climbing between the sheets as he reappeared.

"Close your eyes" he said firmly, approaching the bed. "Your trainin' is about to begin."

"Training?"

"When I told you I was gonna teach you things, I didn't mean just about horses."

She stared up at him, a deep moan escaping her lips.

"Uh-huh, that's what I thought. You may act like a little Miss Bossy Britches, but you've been waitin' for a man to take charge like this for a long time, haven't you Nickie?"

"I guess," she stammered, trying to come to terms with the dominant cowboy promise. "I mean, I'm just starting to realize…"

"You said you were bored. You might feel many things in the comin' days, but bored won't be one of them. Close your eyes."

She suddenly spotted a blindfold in his hand. Her stomach flipped, and a rush of moisture flowed through her sex.

"Deep breaths," he murmured, placing it over her eyes. "We're just startin."

"I'm so excited," she panted. "It sounds like such a lame word, but it's how I feel."

"Lay back and be still for a minute. I've gotta couple of things to do."

"How can I be still?"

Abruptly grabbing her hip, he flipped her over and landed three hard swats.

"Ow, ooh, that hurt."

"That's what happens when you don't do as you're told or you question my instructions. Got it?"

"Yes."

"Yes, Sir," he said firmly. "Next time you forget, you know what will happen."

"Yes, Sir."

"Do as I said. Lie back and be quiet."

Though her bottom was stinging yet again, and her pulse raced, she had never felt so alive, but hearing him move the pillows around the bed caught her attention.

"The pillows are next to you. Place yourself over them so your hips are raised, then spread your arms and legs."

Reaching out in the dark she found the pillows, managed to push them under her hips, then heart pumping as she wondered what would follow, she silently waited.

"What did I tell you to do?"

"Oh, sorry, Sir," she gasped, immediately splaying herself out.

A soft, thick rope circled one ankle, then the other, and she felt the tug as they were secured to what she assumed were the legs of the bed, but when he brought her wrists above her head and tied them together, she uttered a small cry.

"Too tight? I don't wanna hurt you."

"Yes, Sir."

"Is that better?"

"Much, thank you, Sir."

"You're now completely helpless and at my mercy," he murmured, running his fingertips down her spine. "Tell me everything you feel, and don't hold back."

"I'm almost afraid to say how much I love being like this. No-one has ever done anything like it."

"What else?" .

"It's embarrassing having my ass so high. I feel really exposed."

"You are, and in a minute I'm going to examine you."

"You're going to what?"

"I'm going to let that slide, but you only get one of those. Remember, you don't question me. Next time you'll get a very hard swat. The idea of me examining you—it's a turn on—but it also makes you feel what, Nickie?"

"Not scared but weird and, uh, hot."

"If I touch between your legs I'm sure I'll find a very wet pussy," he muttered, climbing on to the bed behind her. "Just as I thought," he continued, pushing his fingers into her sex. "Now I'm going to take a very close look."

His comment brought a fresh flush across her face, but burying her head into the thick, down comforter, she couldn't deny the erotic charge rippling through her veins.

"How lovely you are," he murmured, separating her pussy lips with his thumbs. "So swollen and slick, and your lips are so pink. It makes me want to do all kinds of things to you, wicked things, but I'm going to start with something simple."

Every nerve in her body fired as she felt him leave the bed, but he returned a moment later, and hearing a soft hum, she held her breath. It could mean only one thing.

"Recognize this sound?"

"Yes, Sir."

"Are you ready to be teased?"

"Ooh, yes, Sir. I'm ready for anything."

"That's a very brave thing to say."

As he placed the vibrator against her inflamed sex, she immediately wriggled against it.

"Nope!" he said sternly, pulling it away. "I'll decide on the pressure. Stay still or I'll tighten the ropes and spank your ass hard. Got it?"

"Yes, Sir," she bleated, wondering how she'd ever be able to remain motionless with the tantalizing toy pressed against her pussy.

"Here it comes."

As he touched the bulbous head of the vibrating dildo against her clit, she let out a low moan and clenched her fists. Though she ached to squirm, she managed to fight the urge.

"Good. You want it stronger?"

"Yes, yes, please, Sir," she gasped. "If you think so, I mean, yes, I do. Sir, I don't know what to say."

"Yes, please, Sir was correct."

Turning up the speed and holding it in place, he picked up the condom he'd left on the bed. Ripping it open with his teeth, he slid it over his turgid cock, placed himself at her entrance and plunged into her depths. Crying out her surprise, her fingers curled into fists as he began thrusting with hard, fast strokes.

"Sir, I'm so close," she wailed. "Please, Sir, please let me come?"

Quickly pulling out, he switched off the vibrator.

"Ooh, Sir," she moaned woefully, "please...please..."

"Don't worry, if you're a good girl I'll grant your wish, but first I've gotta paint your sassy cheeks."

She almost asked what he meant, but she caught herself, and a moment later he rested what felt like a small piece of leather against her cheeks.

"Spankin'," he said, gliding the thin narrow strap over her bottom, "can be for punishment or pleasure. You've had the punishment, so now...," he continued, his voice trailing off as he lightly danced the leather against her skin. "Talk to me, Nickie, how does this feel?"

"I love it," she panted breathlessly. "I want to wriggle. Please, Sir, may I?"

"Not tonight. It's trainin'. You've gotta learn to listen, but one day soon I'll let you dance your ass for me. Right now stay very still. I'm gonna move this to your pussy."

She wanted to protest, but he began flicking it against her sex. She froze, but suddenly the sting transformed into an prickling, erotic heat .

"Now you're feelin' it," he murmured, as she arched her back and let out a euphoric cry.

"Yes, Sir, it's...ooooh...so intense but so..."

He paused, then raising the small leather strap, he let it fly with a powerful lash across the center of her bottom.

"Oww—oh, Sir..."

"Just a taste of what you'll get if you don't do as I say. Are clear?"

"Yes, Sir. Very clear. Crystal clear."

But her focus was still between her legs.

Her pussy pulsed with scintillating burn, and all she could think about was her craving for his cock and the return of the vibrator. Then suddenly, like the answer to a prayer, she heard the heavenly buzzing sound.

"Now, Nickie, you can have your pleasure," he declared, pressing the dildo against her clit and sliding his cock back inside her.

"Thank you, Sir," she mewled, then groaned loudly as the sensations tingled through her pussy.

Fucking her with slow, measured strokes, occasionally pausing to enjoy the sensations from the vibrator, he held himself at bay until she cried out her plea.

"Sir, please may I come? Please, Sir?"

"You begged so beautifully," he growled, accelerating his strokes, "yep, come and come hard."

He knew it would be a powerful orgasm, and even as he'd given his blessing, her pussy was grabbing his cock and her howls had begun. Riding her with gusto, delicious spasms jerked his cock, and prickling needles surged through his body.

His climax began to wane, but Nickie's scintillating spasms continued to hold them in their grip. Wave after shimmering wave rippled through her, but as she felt the pressure against her clit easing, the convulsions began to dissipate, and letting out a series of whimpers her body fell limp.

Grabbing a tissue from the nightstand and quickly removing the condom, he slipped from the bed and untied her ropes, then crawling beside her, he removed her blindfold and wrapped her into his arms.

"You okay, sugar?"

"I've never been this okay in my life," she softly mewled. "I feel like I'm in a divine dream."

"You are, we both are, now let yourself drift off to sleep."

As she felt the delicious darkness descend, a fleeting thought crossed her mind. She'd tell him in the morning.

Everything.

She had to.

* * *

Sitting in the cocktail lounge of the Hillsboro Hotel, a dark-haired man ordered a second martini and checked his watch. It was past midnight. His table gave him an unobstructed view of the front doors. He'd already cruised the parking area and found Nicole's Lexus SUV. Wherever she was, someone else was driving.

Sipping his second drink, he glanced up at the television over the bar. It was an old James Bond film, and as he watched, he was reminded there was more than one way to find out if someone had gone out all night.

Rising to his feet, his vigil no longer necessary, he walked to the elevators.

# CHAPTER THIRTEEN

Nickie was woken from a deep sleep by Beau's breath in her ear, and his hand urgently kneading her breasts.

"I have to give these beauties far more attention," he whispered. "They've been sadly neglected."

"Mmmm," she purred, slowly blinking open her eyes. "It's marvey to wake up all warm and cuddly with you."

"Marvey? What kinda word is marvey?"

"My kind of word," she muttered as he moved his lips down her chest and began drawing her nipples into his mouth.

"I'm gonna enjoy gettin' to know you two."

"They're going to love that."

"Just as well," he murmured, gripping both in his hands, "cos I'm gonna have me a titty breakfast."

"You are so bad."

"I hope you're not complainin'."

"Not even close."

"Good. Now leave me alone. These twins here are callin' my name."

Closing her eyes and letting out a happy sigh, she sank into heavenly attention, and as he licked and nuzzled and sucked and tongued, she could feel her needful wetness build between her legs. Though she bleated her pleasure, and occasionally begged him to touch her pussy, completely engrossed in consuming her breasts, he remained deaf to her entreaties.

"I can't stand it," she finally gasped. "You have to touch me or I'll go mad."

"Is that right?" he said leisurely, raising his head. "Hmm, well, I don't want the men in the white coats to take you away, so let's see what I can do."

Stretching across the bed to his nightstand, he searched in his drawer for a condom, finally finding one hidden in the very back.

"I'd better buy a truckload of these today," he mumbled, tearing open the packet.

"I'm on the pill."

"I'll keep that in mind," he said with a grin as he slipped it on. "Where were we? Oh, yeah. You were sayin' somethin' about wantin' your pussy touched. I might just oblige you."

"You can be such a beast."

"I don't know about a beast," he glowed, "but I sure as hell can be an animal."

Kneeling up between her legs, and pulling her pelvis into his, he teased her entrance with his cock, then snaked it home.

"Damn, you feel good," he said huskily. "I'm so horny this is gonna be quick, but don't you worry. I'm gonna fuck you hard and not stop 'til you come."

"I swear, I could climax just from the things you say."

His thrusts began in earnest, growing in speed and power until she was gasping, clutching the sheets and calling his name.

"That's it sugar, you come for me big, real big."

Holding himself back, he watched her gasp and utter her cries of release before he allowed himself to surrender, then closing his eyes he moaned loudly as his cock joyfully erupted. Moments later, as she rested against him, he held her tightly inhaling her scent.

"Now that's how to start a mornin' right," he panted, trying to calm his pounding heart. "I was thinkin', how about we go out to breakfast? I know this great little spot on the other side of the lake, then we can head on up to your house. I wanna take another look now that you wanna change things."

"How can you make love like you're an olympic sprinter," she mumbled breathlessly, "and be talking work thirty-seconds later. I can hardly move."

"Then I guess I'd better get you into shape. You're gonna have to keep up with me."

"I'm not sure I'll survive."

"If it looks like you're about to keel over I'll give you mouth-to-mouth."

"Why am I not reassured?"

"Gettin' back to the house, we can call Geoff when we're there and tell him about your new ideas. I can have a crew together by midweek, assumin' they're not all workin'. Even if they are I'm sure I can rustle up some casual laborers. Most of the tough stuff's been done."

"My hero," she sighed shifting her head and gazing up at him.

"How are you feelin' this mornin'? Besides bein' tuckered out from my wake up call," he added with a chuckle.

"Fine, except my legs hurt from my ride on Trixie. I'm feeling muscles I never knew I had."

"Yep, ridin' will do that, but you'll soon get past it."

"What about you?"

"Me? Real good."

"Me too," she said softly, worried if she told him about the rest of her life it would ruin everything.

"Whoa, girl, what's goin' on with you? You look sad all of sudden."

"I was just thinking about...stuff. Nothing I want to talk about. Let's take a shower and go, I'm starving."

"Nickie, there's somethin' goin' on with you, and you've gotta tell me at some point."

"You're right, and I will, I promise."

"You can tell me anythin'. I might not like it, but I'll still try to understand and do what I can to help."

"Thank you for saying that," she murmured with a sigh. "I hope you feel that way when I tell you. I guess I just have to pluck up the courage."

"Hey, the worst that can happen is I might spank your butt."

"Good grief! Everything begins and ends with spanking my butt."

"Yep, and you'd better get outta bed before I take it into my head to do just that."

Hugging him tightly and kissing him on the cheek, they slipped from the sheets and padded into the bathroom.

* * *

A short time later, Beau was taking her on a short tour of some out-of-the-way shopping spots, then rolled into the parking lot of the comfortable eatery by the lake. The place was hidden from the road by tall trees, and in spite of a sign on the main highway, they rarely had strangers wander in. Sitting outside on the patio, enjoying the view and warm weather, Beau introduced her to a few locals at neighboring tables.

"I love it here," she declared as the waitress took their orders. "Everyone is so friendly."

"I lived in Dallas for a while, worked for a big-time trainer there but I had to get out. I understand the lure of it, the money an' all, but I make a decent livin' here, and I prefer a friendly town over a big city. The worst thing that happens around here is kids on bikes on the horse trails."

"It's so peaceful. I don't think I'm ever going back."

"Really?"

She stared back at him, a deer in headlights.

"You okay?"

"I didn't mean to say that, it just slipped out," she breathed, her face reddening.

"The house you're buildin', you said it's a second home. Has that changed?"

"I, uh, I've been wanting to move for a while, and yeah, I want it to be permanent, but I'm not sure how I can make that happen."

"Because?"

"Um, family stuff. My dad would have an absolute cow, and, uh, there's something else."

"Like?"

"Like, is it okay if we just eat our breakfast first? I'll tell you when we're up at the house. There are too many people around us and I'll probably get upset."

"Sure, later is fine, and I'll help if I can."

"You can't, but thanks," she muttered. "You'll understand later. I'm sorry, things are feeling weird now and I don't want them to be, that's why I didn't say anything earlier."

"Things aren't weird, it's just that there's somethin' we need to talk about and it's on your mind. Here comes our breakfast, this'll cheer you up. Wait 'til you taste the potatoes."

"Let me know if you need anything else," the waitress said, placing their dishes in front of them, then topping up their coffee mugs, she walked away.

"Oh, my, God, you're right," Nickie exclaimed as she took a bite. "They're fantastic."

"Now you know why I drive all the way around the lake to come here?"

The mood lifted, and knowing the subject would bring a smile to her face, he turned the conversation back to his horses.

"I'm havin' some people arrive tomorrow to try out a couple I have for sale. If you promise to behave and be as quiet as a church mouse, you're welcome to come and watch."

"You're not selling Trixie, are you?"

"No, definitely not Trixie. She's a sweet trail girl who will stay with me for the rest of my days."

"Whew, you scared me."

"You don't know much about western ridin', do you?"

"Not a clue, but I love to watch the show jumpers and dressage horses. To be honest, I don't care what kind of riding I do, I just want to do it."

"I know. It was written all over your face," he said with a grin. "Huh, it looks like you weren't hungry at all."

She stared down at her empty plate.

"Not at all, and the food, no flavor and overcooked," she declared in mock seriousness. "I don't think I'll come back."

"Probably just as well."

"Why do you say that?"

"Cos if that's how much you eat when you're not hungry and don't like the food," he said, raising his eyebrows, "I can't imagine how much you'd put away if it tasted good and you were ready to eat."

"Ha, ha. Very funny."

"Let's get up to your house and see if we can figure out the changes you have in your head."

"I want it to be like yours," she said adamantly.

"I'm sure we can make that happen," he said, rising to his feet. "Close anyway."

As they wandered out to the truck, though Nickie wasn't looking forward to telling Beau her secret, she no longer dreaded it. She believed he'd be supportive and understanding. As he drove Betsy back toward town, she was relaxed enough to enjoy the beauty of the mountains surrounding her, and the crystal clear water shimmering in the sun. Turning onto her street, and up the driveway to her half-built house, a frown crossed her brow.

"You know what's strange?" she muttered, as Beau brought the truck to a stop. "I'm looking at this house, and I don't even like it now. It's so, what's the word, cold. You were right, it doesn't suit this area at all. I'm sounding like a broken record, but I want it to be warm and inviting like yours."

"I'm so happy to hear you say that, and we'll make it happen."

"Whenever I come here—to the lake, I mean—after a couple of days I feel different, better. This visit, being with you, riding Trixie, wearing jeans and boots, I feel like a different person."

"You're certainly different from the woman I met," he declared, "and you know what else?" he continued, as they climbed from the truck. "You don't have to worry about messin' up your shoes walkin' into the house."

"This is true," she giggled as she stepped through the dirt patch where the patio was supposed to be.

Wandering into the expansive open space, Beau began pointing out where she could easily separate the area into rooms without losing the sense of flow.

"This is going to be so much better," she said happily. "I just love it."

"Yep, I reckon so too, and if we put in a natural brick fireplace—"

"Yes! Brilliant! I would love that. It's perfect, and we could...wait..what's that? Is that a car?"

"Sure sounds like it. Are you expectin' company?"

"No. Are you?"

"Nope!"

A cold chill crackling down her spine, Nickie turned and ran to the front of the house, then stared in disbelief as the black Mercedes braked to a sharp stop.

"Fuck!"

Her exclamation had been a whisper, but Beau had walked up behind her.

"Nice car," he remarked as the tall, dark-haired, well-dressed man stepped from the SL65 and strode towards them. "I'm guessin' you know who that fella is. He sure doesn't look real happy."

"No. Uh, Beau," she mumbled, a quiver in her voice. "Beau, no matter what he says, don't react, okay? Don't let him provoke you. I'll explain everything, I promise. Please, please trust me."

"Okay. Don't worry. I won't draw any conclusions until we talk."

The stranger was treading carefully through the wide patch of dirt, but paused halfway, raising his head.

"Well, well, so this is your so-called vacation home," he said scornfully. "Interesting front entrance. What do you call this? Patio Au Natural?"

"What are you doing here?" she demanded.

"What do you think, little girl, I've come to take you home," he said brusquely, walking through the rest of the dirt and stepping up into the house. "You're very bad, staying out all night."

"How do you know I've—"

"James Bond, my dear. I put a little piece of string in your door jamb last night, and guess what? It's still there."

"What I do with my time is none of your business!"

"I suppose you think you'll be her new contractor," the man said, ignoring her and staring at Beau.

"I am her new contractor."

"Not for long. Come on, Nicole, we're leaving."

"I'm not going anywhere with you," she spat, "go fuck yourself."

"I don't know who you are," Beau said calmly, stepping between them, "but I believe takin' someone against their will is called kidnappin', and that's a felony."

"You're right, you don't know who I am, how rude of me," the man said, raising one eyebrow. "My name is Gerald Harris, and Nicole is my wife."

## CHAPTER FOURTEEN

Thanks to Nickie's warning, Beau had prepared himself, and when the slick, rude stranger made his declaration, Beau had been able to hide his shock.

"Then I guess I'd best leave you two alone so you can talk," Beau said calmly, "but husband or not, you still can't be takin' someone against their will. If she doesn't wanna go with you, we're gonna have a problem."

Beau could see Gerald Harris sizing him up. They were about the same height and build, and while Beau thought he was probably in better shape than the angry city slicker standing in front of him, it was difficult to judge the man's body under his loose jacket.

"Nickie, I think you two need some privacy, but I'll be close by," Beau promised. "Give a holler if you need me."

As he turned to face her, their eyes met. He read her silent plea to stay, but giving her a reassuring wink, he ambled past her. She watched him for a moment, fighting the temptation to call him back, but Gerald began to speak.

"Come on now, Nicole, be reasonable," he said, his voice as smooth as velvet. "You know you have to come home with me, and I miss you, baby."

"You miss me? You don't seriously expect me to believe that, do you? And I'm not your baby! Just leave, Gerald. I'm not going anywhere with you."

"I'm afraid I can't do that. I promised your father I'd bring you home, and that's exactly what I'm going to do. I want to try again. You know we belong together."

"You shouldn't make promises you can't keep," she exclaimed, "and belong together? What the hell are you talking about? We've never belonged together. Where is all this coming from? I told you I'm filing for a divorce and that's the end of it. Give it up, Gerald."

Listening to the   argument as he made his way across the room, Beau surreptitiously lifted his phone from his pocket and texted Tyler.

**At Nickie's house on Viewpoint. Come quick. Bring George.**

**Ten four.**

Relief flooded his body, but as he slipped the phone back into his pocket, he heard Nickie's plaintive cry for help. Spinning around, he was horrified to see   Gerald dragging her from the house towards his car. Though yelling and struggling furiously, she was no match for Gerald's strength. Pulse ticking up as he marched towards them, he had no desire to fight the man, but he would if he had to.

"Hey, Gerry, the thing is," Beau exclaimed as he approached, "if you don't let her go I'm gonna have to hurt you, and I'd rather not do that. It's not in my nature."

"It's Gerald, and why don't you go kick some shit, cowboy."

Beau paused, put his hands on his hips, and purposefully looked around.

"I said, why don't you go kick some shit," Gerald repeated, raising his voice.

"Hmm," Beau frowned, "I'd like to oblige but I don't see any shit here to kick."

"Let me go you fucking bastard," Nickie screeched, yanking her arm back as hard as she could.

To her surprise she managed to loosen Gerald's grip. Seizing the opportunity, raising her booted foot and landed a hard kick against his shins.

"You fucking bitch!"

The surprise attack enabled her to jerk free, and able to sprint across the dirt patch in the stable footwear, she made it safely to Beau's side.

"You've both got potty mouths," Beau calmly remarked as Nickie panted breathlessly next to him. "Is that where you got that habit from, Nickie? This charmin' husband of yours?"

"You are such a fucking brat," Gerald hissed. "You're going to be sorry you did that."

"Yep, she can be a brat," Beau agreed, "but she's gettin' better, aren't you Nickie?"

"Her name is Nicole, Nicole Harris, as in *Mrs.* Nicole Harris," Gerald snarled moving towards them. "You need to mind your own fucking business. Nicole, get in that fucking car."

"No! I told you, I'm not going anywhere with you and you can't fucking kidnap me."

Pausing his step and lowering his gaze, Gerald scanned the area around him. Sensing the man was looking for a weapon, Beau glanced at the ground. A lead pipe sat between them, but it was closer to Nickie's furious husband.

"Okay, now I'm going to get serious," Gerald warned, lunging forward and snatching it up. "Nicole, you get in that car or this cowboy is going to get his head bashed in."

"No, please, don't," she pleaded. "Okay, okay, I'll go with you."

"Nickie, you stay right where you are," Beau said sternly.

"But he's got a lead pipe. He'll kill you."

"You know what'll happen if you don't do what I'm askin'," he said with a grin.

"I don't know what the hell you're smiling about," Gerald snarled, lifting the pipe in the air and striding forward, "but I'm going to wipe that shit-eating smirk off your face."

"You honestly think you can get the better of me with that oversized toothpick?" Beau asked, wishing Tyler would arrive. "Trust me, you'll be much better off if you climb back in that fancy car of yours and high-tail it outta here."

"You don't know me, dirtbag," Gerald grunted, continuing to walk menacingly forward. "Believe me, I'm not some office boy."

"Now that's a shame," Beau muttered, hearing a car turn up the driveway. "I thought I was gonna have some fun, but it looks like I won't have the time."

Suddenly charging up to the front of the house, a squad car came to a screeching halt behind the Mercedes. Jumping out and pulling his gun, Tyler aimed the lethal weapon at Gerald.

"Drop the pipe, lie on the ground and stretch your arms out."

As he spoke, another officer emerged from the car and lumbered forward. The man was huge, and the sight of the Goliath in uniform scared Gerald almost as much the gun pointed at him.

"Sir, lie on the ground, arms above your head," Tyler demanded, taking a step towards him.

"What? Give me a break," Gerald retorted. "I've put the pipe down. Can't you just handcuff me like this?"

"Are you resisting arrest, Sir?"

"Hell, no," Gerald said hastily. "I just don't want to lie in all that dirt and gravel. This suit wasn't cheap."

"Sir, I'll tell you one more time, hit the ground with your arms above your head or I'll book you for resisting arrest."

"Sonofabitch!" Gerald growled, slowly dropping to his knees. "This is bullshit."

"All the way down! Arms out at your sides."

"You'll be sorry you're treating me like this," Gerald muttered, stretching out on his stomach. "I know people. Important people. You'll be directing fucking traffic by this time tomorrow, if you have a job at all."

"George, cuff him and read him his rights," Tyler directed, holstering his gun and moving quickly across the dirt patch into the house. "Hey, Beau, Nickie. Are you two okay?"

"Thank God you came," Nickie exclaimed, clinging to Beau. "How did you know?"

"Ask your cowboy," Tyler replied. "That was a wise move, Beau."

"I knew that guy was trouble, and I didn't wanna take any chances with Nickie here."

"But I don't understand," Nickie muttered. "I didn't see or hear you make any phone calls."

"I sent a quick text, but you're shaking," Beau said gently, putting his arm around her shoulders. "Take a deep breath. It's over."

"When he picked up the pipe..."

"Yeah, that was a scary moment, but look, the jolly green giant is takin' Gerald's sorry butt to the squad car," Beau joked, trying to lighten the mood. "Tyler, how long can you hold him?"

"If you press charges, until his arraignment in the morning."

"I want him outta here, so forget the charges, but can you keep him locked up for a couple of hours?"

"That won't be a problem."

"What about his car?" Nickie asked. "Does it have to stay here?"

"Don't worry, I'll have it impounded, but you're white as a sheet. You need to go someplace and catch your breath."

"I agree, and I owe you one," Beau said, shaking his hand. "Thanks so much."

"Hey, you don't owe me anything, it's my job. I'm just glad I was close by, though in this town I'm never far from anywhere."

"Nickie, are you ready to go back to the ranch?" Beau asked. "I think we could both use a cup of coffee."

"Yes, please," she said with a heavy sigh, "and Beau, I'm so sorry this happened, I had no idea he'd show up. He's never even been here."

"We'll talk about that later," he murmured as they began walking from the house.

"You two take care," Tyler said, moving quickly ahead of them. "I'll make sure that creep knows to keep his distance."

Beau had parked the truck to the side of the driveway, and as they passed the police car, Nickie glanced at Gerald sitting in the back seat.

"That's exactly where he belongs, the bastard."

"And he looked like such a nice fella when he first arrived," Beau said sarcastically, as Gerald glowered at him through the window.

"He's about as nice as a rattlesnake."

They climbed into the truck, and maneuvering it around the two vehicles, Beau headed down the driveway. As he turned onto the street, he reached across and took her hand.

"Nickie, it's probably not a good idea for you to stay in that hotel. Gerald, seems like the determined type."

"He is, very," she said grimly. "He won't give up, believe me."

"I can ask Amy to pack your stuff and bring it to the ranch, or we can swing by the hotel and pick it up."

"Are you saying I can stay with you?"

"Of course!" he exclaimed. "I'm gonna watch out for you until this is settled, and if you're not under my roof, how am I gonna do that? I wouldn't sleep a wink with you at that hotel and that man runnin' around. You'll be doin' me a favor."

"Beau, you're the best," she said gratefully, pecking him on the cheek. "He won't know where to find me if I'm at the ranch. Let's go to the hotel. I'll check out, and I won't go anywhere until I know he's left town."

"Sounds like a plan!"

"Oh, my car! If it's in the parking lot and Gerald sees it, he'll stick around."

"Of course. I'd forgotten about that too. Just to be on the safe side, you can park it at the back of the barn. On the off-chance he finds out who I am and where I live, it won't be seen if he decides to be a nuisance and show up at the door."

"I should have told you about him," Nickie murmured, dropping her eyes. "I'm sorry. I just, uh, didn't know where to start, and I didn't want to spoil things."

"I've gotta admit I was surprised, but obviously he's history and has been for a while. Once we're home, though, I wanna hear the whole story."

"I want to tell you, but, uh, you might not like it."

"Forewarned is forearmed," he said with a grin. "I'm pretty sure I'll be able to handle it."

Staring out the window as they passed the lake, she prayed he was right. It wasn't a pretty story.

# CHAPTER FIFTEEN

Beau had no doubt Gerald Harris would soon uncover the name and address of the cowboy who had foiled him, and he wasn't about to take any chances. The moment he arrived back at the ranch he searched out Ben and Jeb, gave them Gerald's description, and told them if the man came on the ranch to throw him off the property.

Sitting at the kitchen table with a cup of tea and chocolate cake, Nicole was starting to feel like herself again. With the Lexus parked behind the barn, and the two muscled ranch hands alerted and ready to protect her, Nickie felt safe and reassured.

"Are you about ready to tell me about this husband of yours?" Beau asked. "If not, it's okay."

"I am, and I swear I was about to fill you in right before he showed up, but now I don't know where to start?"

"At the beginnin', but keep it simple."

"The beginning," she said thoughtfully. "Almost a year ago I had a drunken roll in the hay with him and ended up pregnant."

"Whoa! Are you tellin' me—"

"No, no, I don't have a child. I lost the baby shortly after the wedding. I didn't want to marry him, but I come from a line of old-fashioned Italians, and the pressure—I can't begin to describe it," she exclaimed rolling her eyes. "Gerald was thrilled of course, claimed he loved me to pieces, but I was a mess. After the miscarriage I was an even worse mess."

"Why didn't you just get a quick divorce?"

"You think everything is so black and white," she muttered, shaking her head. "Maybe in your world it is. Gerald has bagged himself one of the heirs to the Pantera Jeans company. Yeah, he has his own money, but now he'll have even more."

Her voice had cracked, and Beau realized she really was desperate.

"What about your mom and dad? Surely they'll help."

"My mom and I don't get along at all, and my dad, I know he loves me, but he believes marriage is for life. I told you, old-fashioned. The thing is, Gerald's family has been friends with mine forever. My brothers, John and Adam, are super close to Gerald and his three brothers. It's just so fucking incestuous."

"How is that possible Gerald's never been here?"

"He spends almost every weekend on golfing excursions, so I decided to take off as well. The minute I came over the hill and saw the lake and town, I fell in love. Right then I decided to build a home here. An escape. I didn't tell anyone. My biggest mistake was hiring a city contractor. I'm a Pantera. Somehow it got out."

"So he confronted you."

"It was bad, and about the same time I lost the contractor and couldn't find another one. I was at my wits end. Last week we had a huge fight, and I told him if he didn't divorce me I'd make up stories about him and sell them to the tabloids. I'd never do something like that, but it just suddenly popped into my head. He went ballistic, and I packed a suitcase and came out here."

"Ah. That's why you're in such a hurry to finish the house."

"I'm done with everything and everyone. I don't want to work for the family business anymore, but most of all, I have to get away from that neanderthal, " then pausing, she wistfully added, "and now I want horses."

Leaning back in his chair, Beau sipped his tea.

"I'm gonna say something you're not gonna like," he began slowly. "Maybe you're attracted to me 'cos I'm different. I'm a cowboy and live a simple life on a ranch in a small town."

Her eyes gazed back at him, and finishing her tea, she rose from the table and wandered to the kitchen window.

"Maybe," she murmured, trying to control the tremble in her voice as she gazed out at the horses. "It could be all of those things, or none of those things. Attraction happens for all kinds of reasons, but I can tell you this. The way I feel when you hold me, when you kiss me, it's...it's like nothing I can describe. It's real, you're real, you're in my heart, and if you don't know that—but now Gerald's here, and everything's crazy..."

Her voice trailed off, and as her tears began to spill, Beau jumped from his chair and walked quickly across the room to hug her.

"Hey, this is real for me too."

"I'm sorry I didn't tell you about Gerald, honestly," she sniffled, "but for the first time in forever I've been happy."

"We'll figure this out together, I promise."

"I'm scared, Beau, I'm scared of Gerald and my family."

"It's gonna crinkle out. My old man always said, *watch and wait and just let things develop*."

"Beau?" she murmured, pulling back and staring up at him, "please can you take me upstairs? I need you."

Moving his hands into her hair, he curled her long tresses through his fingers.

"I need you too, Nickie."

* * *

Slipping between the sheets, Nickie snuggled into Beau's body, closed her eyes and let out a sigh.

"I love this," she whispered. "There's no other place I'd rather be than right here."

"Yeah, I feel the same, but you've been a bad girl."

"I have?"

"You've been using bad language again," he continued, propping himself up on an elbow to gaze down at her. "It's a habit that needs to be broken, and I'm gonna help you do just that."

"But—"

"No more buts—unless you're talkin' about your beautiful backside," he said with a grin. "Don't worry, I'll consider the circumstances, but your ass is gonna get some attention."

Her eyes sparkled up at him. It had worked. He'd distracted her from the drama. Lowering his lips to her breasts he nibbled and sucked, eliciting moans of pleasure, then kissed his way up her chest and neck to languidly devour her mouth.

"Roll on to your stomach," he said softly. "Understand?"

"It's not rocket science," she quipped with a sassy grin.

"We're in one of those moods, are we?"

"Apparently."

"Your choice," he retorted, raising one wicked eyebrow. "Do as you're told. Roll over and close your eyes."

Shifting on to her stomach, she stared over her shoulder to see him swing his leg over her body, but he was facing her feet.

"I can feel you watching me," he declared. "Lay your head on the pillow and do as I said. I won't be happy if I have to fetch the blindfold."

Dropping her face into the soft comfort of the goose-down, she shut her eyes and waited. She could feel him sitting lightly on the small of her back, and a moment later his hands began roaming across her bottom.

"Why am I gonna spank you?"

"Because of my bad language."

"Which was?"

"Using the word fuck."

His hand swatted down.

"Ow!"

"What was it again?"

"Fuck."

Another stinging smack.

"Ouch."

"Tell me again?"

"Beau...please..."

"That wasn't the correct answer," he scolded, landing three hard smacks to each cheek in rapid succession. "What was the word?"

"Fuck, and I'm sorry."

"You think you might say that word in front of me again?" he demanded, raining a flurry of hot slaps.

"No, no, I won't, I promise," she gasped. "Oh, I won't, I won't."

"If you do, you know what will happen, right?"

"Yes, Sir, ow, ow," she bleated, trying to wriggle in vain, "and I'll get the dumbest girl of the year award."

"Get on your back," he ordered, chuckling as he slid off her body and stretched out next to her.

"You spanked me hard."

"Not that hard," he said, bringing her into his arms, "and I told you if you used that word again I'd punish you. You shouldn't be surprised. I always keep my promises."

"I think you just like spanking me."

"Well, there is that," he admitted, "but Nickie, that wasn't hard. I spanked you just enough to deliver the message. Quit complainin' or I'll start up again, and isn't there something else you need?"

"Yes, please," she said softly, spreading her legs and moving her hand to his crotch.

Roaming his hand across her breasts and down to her pussy, his fingers between her lips.

"Mmm, so wet. Dammit, I'm outta condoms. I should've picked some up at the hotel."

"You don't have to worry. I'm on the pill. My days of taking chances are over."

"It's been a long time since I didn't use a condom," he said thoughtfully. "It's not you I don't trust, it's that man you're married to. I doubt he was golfin' every weekend."

"This is so not romantic," she said with a sigh. "I started sleeping in a separate room with the door locked ages ago hoping he'd give up and let me leave, but you're probably right. I honestly hadn't thought about it."

"I'll pick some up tomorrow, and we can both get tested as well, but in the meantime—"

"In the meantime, may I have the honor of pleasuring you, Sir?" she asked, pushing him on to his back and planting kisses on his chest.

"Since you asked so nicely."

Traveling her lips down his torso, she wrapped her fingers around his thick shaft and lowered her lips to the bulbous head. Suddenly grabbing her hair, he took control and began guiding her movements. A wave of moisture flooded her sex, and letting out a muffled moan, she shifted her position to grind herself against his leg.

"You need to ask permission to do that," he grunted, tugging her head up.

"I can't help it, Sir. Everything you do turns me on."

"Is that your way of askin'?"

"Uh, sorry. Please may I, Sir?"

"Get back to suckin' my cock, but yeah, you can rub yourself against me."

"Thank you, Sir."

Gratefully moving her leg over his muscled thigh, she returned her lips and tongue to his waiting member.

* * *

As the minutes ticked by and Beau's climax began to hover, Nickie's urgent  grinding grew more fervent. Loathe for her to stop, but knowing he'd explode if she didn't, he reluctantly tugged her hair and pulled her off.

"Come and lie next to me," he said huskily.

As she moved up the bed, he positioned her on her back, then kneeling at her side, he gazed at her breasts and took hold of his rigid cock.

"Touch yourself. I wanna see you come."

As she moaned softly and placed her fingers against her clit, he stroked himself with one hand, and tweaked her puckered, cherry nipples with the other.

"I love you towering over me like this," she mewled, gazing up at him. "You're so—"

But his fingers abruptly pinched the inside of her thighs, cutting her off.

"Wider," he growled. "Spread them wider."

Splaying herself out and urgently massaging her small nub, she gasped as his fingers continued to tweak the silky, sensitive skin, then let out a shocked cry as he slapped her where he'd just pinched. The fiery sting blazed hot, but it fed her fever and her orgasm loomed.

"Beau, I'm so close!"

"Let it happen," he grunted, returning his hands to play with her breasts as he jerked his rod.

Squeezing her eyes shut, she let out a wail, and as her body spasmed, his climax rose up and exploded across his hand. The exquisite convulsions sparked through his limbs, and though the climax was brief, it was intense, leaving him breathless and his heart pounding as he fell next to her.

"Beau?"

Momentarily confused and opening his eyes, he realized he'd dropped into nothingness for a moment. The covers were over them, and she was nestling into his body.

"Hey," he crooned, lifting his arm to cradle her.

"Did you pass out? You dropped like a lead balloon, and when I pulled up the bedspread you didn't move."

"Really? Huh, I guess maybe I did for a minute. My heart sure was racin'."

"Is that normal? Now I'm worried."

"Nickie, there's nothin' normal about any of this," he murmured, then softly added, "but that was one helluva climax."

"Me too," she said as a yawn swept her up. "I'm so tired."

"I'm not surprised. We both need a power nap. When we wake up we can go downstairs and I'll rustle us something to eat."

"I can do that."

"You cook? I don't believe it."

"Who said anything about cooking?" she replied with a grin. "I was thinking I'd make a phone call. My treat."

"If I wasn't so tired I think I'd give you a swat for that."

"If I wasn't so tired I'd say, please do. What time is it anyway?"

"Dunno, don't care, and I'm gonna rest now."

But as she nestled into him and closed her eyes, Gerald's angry face danced in her mind's eye. For a brief moment she'd been able to forget, but as a frightening chill pricked her skin, she knew he'd find her, and when he did...

## CHAPTER SIXTEEN

Waking from a sound sleep and finding Nickie still in never-never land, Beau softly slipped from the bed, pulled on his robe and moved downstairs to shower in the guest room. As the hot water splashed over him, he recalled how happy and amazingly confident Nickie had been riding Trixie. She'd given no hint of the drama surrounding her.

Stepping from the stall and searching out a comb to run through his unruly hair, he was delighted to find an unopened packet of condoms in the drawer. Ripping it open and taking out several, he dropped them into his pocket, then wandered into the kitchen and set the coffee to brew. Ambling across to the window to look at his horses, he watched Ben and Jeb driving from paddock to paddock throwing out the hay. In the summer months they lived in the pastures, but it wouldn't be long before winter rolled in and they'd be brought into the barn for the overnight hours.

Moving back to the counter to pour himself a cup of the fresh coffee, the melody of the song he'd started to write floated through his head. Lyrics quickly followed. Walking quickly to his desk, he pulled out the yellow pad and scanned what he'd written.

I don't know where you came from,
I don't know who you are,
I admit to feelin' kinda strange
And I'm likin' it so far,

You're a different kinda woman,
With a different kinda love,
A different kinda something
A naughty Angel from above.

When you're nowhere in sight,
You're living in my head,
I wanna wake up with you against me
I need you in my bed.

You're a different kinda woman,
With a different kinda love,
A different kinda something
A naughty Angel from above.

The remainder of the song raced through his head, and grabbing a pen he sat down and jotted down the words.

You're running fast and running hard
You can escape into my arms,
I'll keep you warm and safe my love,
I'll keep you outta harm.

Sometimes a woman needs a man
to step up and fight her fight.
Ain't no shame in that sweet girl,
Stick with me, I'll make things right.

You're a different kinda woman,
With a different kinda love,
A different kinda something
A naughty Angel from above

He grinned. It was perfect. Returning his pen and pad to the drawer, he headed back to the kitchen knowing one day he'd sing it to her. Opening the pantry to search out a muffin, he abruptly remembered Gina was supposed to be coming by. Rushing to the house phone, he dialed her number, praying he wasn't too late.

"Hey, big boy," she said cheerily. "You're calling early."

"Hey, Gina, thanks for a great lunch yesterday."

"You're welcome. You sound happy. I assume everything went well."

"It did, but—"

"Let me guess, your friend is still there?"

"She is," Beau said with a chuckle. "Am I that transparent?"

"I've known you a long time."

"It's fine if you still wanna come over, and I'd like you to, but she's not up yet so maybe a bit later?"

"Around noon?"

"Yep. Thanks Gina."

"I'm looking forward to meeting her."

"She's, uh, different, but I know you'll like her. See you later."

Retrieving the muffin from the pantry, he settled at the kitchen table, took a bite and sipped his coffee. Though he wanted to show Nickie the rest of the property he wasn't sure if they should leave the house, but his cellphone rang, breaking into his pondering. He checked the screen. The caller was Tyler.

"Hey, Tyler, what's the word?"

"Hi, Beau. I've got good news, and maybe some bad. Gerald Harris has checked out of the hotel and picked up his car from the impound lot. From what I've been told, he raced out of here early."

"That's great," Beau declared, picking up his mug and moving back to the window. "What's the bad news?"

"He booked the Holmby Suite for tonight."

"I don't understand?"

"He used his credit card to hold it, but it's for a guy named Joseph Pantera."

"Aw, shit."

"Is that bad?"

"It could be. Joseph Pantera is either one of Nickie's brothers, or her father. Either one isn't good."

"Sounds like you've got your hands full."

"Now that I think about it, we don't even know if Harris is truly gone," Beau remarked. "He could be anywhere."

"You're right about that, and if he's hell-bent on finding Nickie you won't be hard to track down."

"Can you and your boys keep an eye on this place? Ben and Jeb know to intercept any strangers, but—"

"Say no more," Tyler interrupted. "We'll keep watch."

"Let them know I have some folks comin' to look at some horses this afternoon. Probably not a good idea to be friskin' the customers."

"Not to worry. They know what Gerald Harris looks like and the make and model of his car, but I hope you're showing those horses early."

"What makes you say that?"

"Didn't you know? The winds are coming."

"They are? I haven't watched the news for a couple of days. I vaguely remember the weather report claimin' there was a chance, but nothin' for sure."

"It's more than a chance. They'll be starting late this afternoon and hitting full force overnight and into tomorrow. The latest report says the storm will be a humdinger."

"Dang! I'm so glad you told me. The buyers are comin' around lunchtime so we should be okay, but I'll make sure the barns and the horses are locked up tight after they leave. Thanks, Tyler."

"Beau, uh, before I go," he said tentatively, "maybe I'm crossin' a line here, but, uh, Nickie's a real looker and seems like a great girl but —"

"But I might be gettin' into something maybe I shouldn't," Beau declared, cutting him off.

"You don't really know her."

"True, it's only been a few days since I met her, but I think that horse has left the barn, and I'm not ready to jump outta the saddle, at least, not yet."

"Women!"

"Yeah," Beau said with a rueful chuckle. "Thanks again. Catcha later."

Ending the call, he watched Pepper teasing the other horses, then bucking as they teased him back.

"You want to jump out of the saddle?"

Momentarily paralyzed, and silently cursing himself for not being more careful, he took a deep breath and turned around. Standing just inside the kitchen dressed in the shirt he'd discarded the night before, she took his breath away. She looked unbelievably sexy, but vulnerable and confused.

"Hey," he said softly, moving towards her, "you didn't hear right. I said I'm *not* ready to jump outta the saddle."

"*Yet*, and you said you might be getting into something you shouldn't. I heard you coming down the stairs. I don't blame you. Who would want to take on all my problems? But you're a good guy so you feel like you—"

"Stop right there!"

Placing his phone on the table, he strode quickly forward and placed his hands on her shoulders.

"It's okay," she mumbled staring up at him, "I'll get my things and—"

"Nickie," he said sharply, "what you heard was out of context, and let's face it, you might wanna jump outta the saddle one of these days. Neither of us know what's around the corner, but I'm not goin' anywhere, and I don't want to."

"I've been nothing but trouble since we met, and things are just getting worse. You're probably sorry I ever called you!"

Suddenly ducking away, she turned to run up the stairs, but Beau was too quick. Catching her wrist and spinning her around, he engulfed her in a bear hug.

"Nickie, listen to me! I told you I'm not goin' anywhere, and I meant it."

"I'm too much trouble," she protested, squirming in his hold. "Me and my screwed up life!"

"You can wriggle all you want, but I'm not lettin' you go until you calm down. You're totally overreactin'. I'm crazy about you, don't you get that?"

"Why would you be crazy about me?" she asked mournfully, "I'm nothing but a big mess, and you have this perfect, wonderful life."

Holding her tightly with one arm, he clutched her hair with the other and yanked back her head. Her eyes blazed up at him, but he dropped his lips against hers, pressing fervently, demanding a response.

As the fight began to leave her, his kiss became warm and inviting, soft and luxuriant, tender and loving. Sweeping her up he carried her into the guest room, and laying her on the bed, he sent the buttons flying as he ripped off her shirt.

Dropping his robe and sliding a condom in place, he rested his weight on top of her and snaked his cock into her wet pussy. Wordlessly devouring her, he traveled his lips ardently over her face and neck, pumping with abandon until they were both lost in their mutual climaxes and crying out their orgasmic euphoria.

* * *

Nestling against him and catching her breath, she wanted to say something, but she wasn't sure what, and before she could find the words, Beau shifted his body to gaze down at her.

"I want you to listen to me very carefully," he murmured, still slightly panting. "If you're not sure about something, ask, don't go jumpin' to conclusions."

"I'm sorry, it was such a scary moment."

"If you ever overhear anything that worries you, I don't care what it is, talk to me."

"Anything?"

"Sure. Why?"

"Um, there is one thing."

"Spit it out."

"All the condoms you seem to have around this place. I mean, how many girls do you, uh, are you—"

"Nickie," he said with a grin, "I'm a guy. I have condoms, and like I said I don't have sex without 'em. But to answer your question, when I took a shower down here this mornin' I found an unopened box in the bathroom drawer. I totally forgot they were there."

"You don't have a harem, or a special someone?"

"Hell, no, I don't have a harem," he exclaimed. "I mean, I have a couple of friends who call me from time to time, but I always have condoms handy. My momma used to say, it's better to have it and not need it, than need it and not have it."

"She said that to you about condoms?" Nickie asked, wide-eyed. "I can see your dad, maybe, but—"

"No," he replied, laughing out loud, "she said that about things like, if I was headin' out and didn't have a jacket, *Beau,* she'd say, *it's better to have it..."*

"Ooh, I see."

"Sure is good to see that smile back on your face."

"Uh, you didn't answer the second part of my question. No-one special?"

"There is now," he murmured, leaning in and brushing her lips in a soft, sweet kiss.

"Good answer," she breathed. "Sorry about my melt down. I get a bit carried away sometimes."

"No kiddin'."

"Who were you talking to?"

"Tyler. He called to tell me Gerald checked out of the hotel and picked up his car from the impound lot. Apparently he left town."

"I should be relieved, but I'm sorry to say, if he's gone it's temporary. What?" she asked gravely, seeing the cloud cross his face.

"I agree," he answered, deciding to tell her about the hotel reservation later. "We can't be sure if he's truly gone or just layin' low, but Tyler and his guys will be cruisin' by the ranch keepin' an eye on things. You'll be safe here."

"I'll be safe anywhere you are," she murmured, curling next to him. "Is there anything on the agenda today?"

"Breakfast, and after that we need to call Geoff about the changes you want. Then I'll start callin' my crew and see who's available. Gina will be swingin' by around noon, and then those folks will be comin' to look at the two horses I told you about."

"Sounds like you're going to be busy. Let me know how I can help, but right now, breakfast, please. I'm starving."

"Why don't you go take a shower and get dressed? By the time you come back down, it'll be ready and waitin'."

"Beau, thank you," she said, lifting her head and kissing him on the cheek. "You've been amazing."

"Hey, thank *you* for sweepin' into my life. Things were startin' to get a bit dull around here. Go on now, or we'll never leave this bed."

"Works for me."

"Go!" he exclaimed, abruptly sitting up and landing a swat.

"Okay, okay."

He was grinning, but as she pulled on his T-shirt and left the room, he let out a heavy sigh. The Devil Wind was on the way, and it was known for blowing in trouble.

## CHAPTER SEVENTEEN

Arriving at the ranch just past noon, Gina noticed an attractive, dark-haired young woman brushing Trixie. The shapely girl wore jeans, a red plaid shirt and paddock boots, but she appeared to be new to horses. Her long hair kept falling across her face, and she was studying the various brushes in the grooming kit. Rolling her vintage jeep to a stop, Gina reached across the seat for one of several baseball caps she kept in her car. Deciding on a red one to match the girl's shirt, she climbed out and looked around for Beau. Not seeing him anywhere, she decided to introduce herself.

"Hi, there, this might help," she offered, approaching Nickie and holding out the hat.

"Oh, great. Thank you. I hardly ever wear a baseball cap, but my hair is driving me crazy."

"I'm Gina, and you're welcome. I live in them."

"Oh, hi, you're Beau's—"

"Chief, cook and bottle washer," Beau declared.

Both startled, they turned in unison to see him walking briskly towards them.

"Hey, Gina, thanks for comin'," he said with a smile, kissing her on the cheek. "I see you've met Nickie. A baseball cap. Of course. I should've thought of that."

"Gina, I have to tell you," Nickie declared, "that cheesecake you made, good grief, you should sell them."

"I'm glad you liked it, and I do. I don't just take care of Beau here, I own a small bakery, but I don't have to do any of the grunge work now, unless I want to. Sometimes I do, then I remember why I hire people."

"I don't understand. If you have a business why do you want to clean houses?"

"I only clean this house, and I love the horses and spending time here, but most of all I love Beau. He needs someone to take care of him, don't you honey?"

"Yes, ma'am. I'd be lost without you."

"Back at ya," she said warmly. "Speaking of which, I need to get inside and see what's what. Good to meet you Nickie. I hope the hat helps."

"You too, and thanks again."

Watching Gina walk up to the house, Nickie gathered up her hair and pulled it through the back of the cap.

"This is perfect," she declared, settling the hat in place. "That was so thoughtful of her, but I don't get the whole house cleaning thing."

"I'll explain later. I know you said you're not hungry, but are you sure you don't want some lunch?"

"Honestly, that breakfast was plenty, and I'm dying to get back on Trixie. See? She's all set."

Beau had suggested a quick lesson on the easy mare before the buyers arrived. Thrilled by the suggestion, Nickie had insisted on getting her ready.

"She looks good. Fetch her saddle. You know the one."

"Me?"

"Yep. You have to know how to saddle a horse if you're gonna learn how to ride."

* * *

Watching from the bay window in the kitchen, Gina had to smile. Beau was crazy about the new woman in his life, and he'd been right, Nickie was different. She was polished and sharp, and though Gina sensed the young woman had a tough edge, Gina had also recognized vulnerability.

"Well, I'd better get started," she muttered. "The clothes won't wash themselves."

Moving into the laundry room and picking up a basket, she headed up to Beau's bathroom, gathered the clothes and towels from the hamper, then decided to strip the bed. She'd just finished when the telephone rang.

"Chapman residence," she declared, picking up the receiver from the phone on the nightstand.

"Is Beau Chapman available?"

A frown crossed her face. The male voice was one she didn't recognize.

"I don't believe he's available. Can you hold a minute please?"

Placing the receiver on the nightstand, she walked quickly to the window and looked across the yard. Beau had taken Nickie to the round pen, but she also noticed Ben and Jeb riding in the arena. Their horses gleamed, and she remembered Beau had said buyers would be arriving around lunchtime. Glancing back to Nickie and Beau, they were laughing and appeared to be having a wonderful time. Gina decided to take a message.

* * *

Beau had just taught Nickie how to neck rein when a truck and trailer rolled down the driveway. He checked his watch. Eleven-forty-five. The buyers were early, but he wasn't surprised. He made it a point to do the same when looking at  horses. It would often result in watching their behavior while being groomed and saddled. He didn't mind, but he would have preferred more time with Nickie.

"At least you can steer now," he said with a smile. "Do you feel confident enough to ride Trixie to the outdoor ring and watch me from the rail?"

"Yes, absolutely. I never want to get off."

"I won't introduce you, and you need to hang back."

"No problem. So…you'll be riding?"

"Yep," he said, opening the gate, "and I'll put on a show just for you."

"Cool. I can't wait."

Trixie fell into step behind him as he strode across to meet the buyers, but Nickie peeled off as they neared the two cowboys waiting by the trailer. Asking the mare to stop at the side of the ring, she watched Jeb and Ben take the horses over to Beau and the visitors.

They talked for a minute, then Beau mounted a copper-colored horse.

A moment later Beau blazed into the ring at a full gallop, then whizzed around two barrels, one set on each end of the arena. She couldn't believe the speed of the horse and Beau's brilliance in the saddle. When he came to an abrupt stop and jumped off, one of the visiting cowboys climbed on board. Though he appeared to ride the horse well, he didn't have the same flair.

There was a short break as Ben and Jeb removed the barrels, and thrilled with what she'd seen, Nickie waited eagerly for the other horse to perform.

Climbing on the shiny black gelding, Beau positioned himself in front of a row of gates. As three heifers were released, the horse darted backwards and forwards to keep one of the cows away from the other two. Beau seemed to do nothing but sit in the saddle. The entire episode lasted only a couple of minutes, but when he'd finished and trotted over to the buyers, Nickie was amazed by what she'd witnessed. The horse had moved so sharply, she couldn't understand how he'd stayed on.

Beau dismounted, and the second cowboy climbed into the saddle. A few minutes later the exercise was repeated with the buyer, and again Nickie was awed by the spectacle.

"That was incredible," she muttered, watching the cowboy head back to the truck and climb off. "Okay, Trixie, will you take me back to the barn, but slowly like you brought me over here?"

Using the neck rein technique she'd just learned, she gave a little cluck, and to her delight, Trixie turned around and ambled towards the stable yard. A gentle breeze danced around them, and when they reached the hitching post Nickie spied leaves scurrying across the ground. Carefully lowering herself from the saddle, she smiled proudly.

"Hey there, we haven't been introduced. I'm Ben," a good looking cowboy declared, jogging up to her. "Beau thought you might need a hand."

"Thanks, I'm Nickie, and yes, this thing's heavy," she remarked as she unbuckled the girth. "The horse that was racing around those barrels, what's his name?"

"That's Chester. The other one's Midnight Run. They're real good."

"They were both amazing. I've never seen anything like that."

"Beau's a great trainer."

"Do you think those guys will buy them?"

"It's their second visit, and those boys didn't pull that trailer here for fun," Ben said with a chuckle, "but Beau's real picky about who gets his horses."

"That doesn't surprise me," she said with a smile, stepping back to give him room as he pulled off the saddle.

"I'll put this on the rack for you, then I have to go finish up," he said, but as he turned to head into the barn, a gust of wind whistled past them. He paused, lifting his eyes to the trees. "Dang. It's comin'."

"What's coming?" Nickie frowned, the tone of his voice unsettling.

"The wind," he replied, walking into the barn. "You don't know about that?"

"Beau told me it can get bad sometimes," she replied, following him inside.

"Yep, and you'll know what that means in just a couple of hours," he said gravely, placing the saddle on its stand. "It's not called the Devil Wind for nothin'."

"That doesn't sound good. How did it get such a scary name?"

"It blows in trouble," he replied grimly "I'd best get back. Real nice meetin' you."

"Thanks for the help."

"Any time," he said with a nod, then marched from the barn.

Grabbing some carrots from a bucket, she ambled outside and looked across at the trailer. Chester and Midnight Run stood quietly munching from hay nets, but Beau and the visitors were nowhere to be seen, then to Nickie's surprise and absolute delight, Trixie lifted her head and nickered.

"Trixie! Do you know me?"

As the mare stared back at her with large brown eyes, Nickie's heart melted.

"I'm supposed to be around horses," she mumbled, stepping forward and feeding Trixie the treat. "I take that back, I want to be around horses, especially you."

"That's good to hear."

Turning around, she found Beau striding up behind her.

"You have a very bad habit of sneaking up on people!"

"I know, and it's taken years of practice," he retorted with a wicked grin.

"Were those buyers impressed? I sure was."

"They're stayin' overnight and comin' back after the wind passes through. They wanna ride some of the trails around here."

"They didn't know the wind was on its way?"

"Nope, they weren't payin' attention to the weather and neither was I. At least I have an excuse. I was distracted by this crazy, short-tempered, sexy, gorgeous girl that came whistlin' into my life."

"That's what I am? An excuse?"

"Hey, it's the truth."

"Don't worry, you can use me as an excuse anytime, but about this wind. Ben said it's called the Devil Wind and it blows in trouble."

"That's what they say. All the horses will be brought into the barn, and from the looks of those trees wavin' around, I wanna take Trixie in now. One less for the boys. Pick up her reins and follow me."

Leading Trixie, she followed him around the corner of the large barn and walked inside. She found herself at the end of a long, wide aisle, and spotted Ben and Jeb busy further down. Stopping at a stall bearing Trixie's name, Beau slid open the door.

"Take her in, remove the bridle slowly like I showed you, then fetch her some hay. It's right over there," he said, pointing to several bales stacked inside a nearby stall.

"Beau, I've never been in a barn, but I've seen pictures, and these stalls look really big," she remarked, carefully taking off Trixie's bridle.

"They're doubles. Bad enough that a horse has to be inside, let alone in a space too small to walk around in. I pulled out the partitions so they have more room. Stalls are usually twelve by twelve, these are twelve by twenty-four."

Gazing into his smoky-blue eyes, smelling the aroma of the barn, and running her hand down Trixie's soft neck, a wave of emotion stirred her heart.

"Beau," she whispered, "I...uh...need a hug."

"Any time," he murmured, stepping up to her.

Leaning against him as he wrapped her up, she heard a gust of wind.

A shiver rippled down her spine.

*It blows in trouble.*

As Ben's words rang through her head, she prayed the trouble wouldn't be in the form of Gerald Harris.

## CHAPTER EIGHTEEN

With the wind picking up, Beau, Ben and Jeb began bringing in the horses. Nickie helped by throwing hay in the stalls, hooking up water buckets in the stalls that didn't have them, then dragging the hose through the barn aisle and filling them. It took almost an hour, and as Beau and Jeb began securing the shutters over the windows, seeing Nickie wrestle a hose that appeared to be a gymnastic python, Ben hurried to her rescue.

"What's wrong with this thing?" she exclaimed as Ben jogged up.

"It fights with all of us," Ben said with a chuckle, taking it from her hands. "The thin ones kink, and that's a real pain, but these thick, expensive ones can be difficult to handle. There, that's done it," he declared, managing to get the last coil around the holder.

"Are you done?" Beau asked as he and Jeb approached.

"I think so," Nickie replied. "I've never done anything like this and I had the best time."

"It was great havin' another pair of hands," Ben said gratefully. "You can come and help out any time."

"Thank you."

"About the schedule," Beau began. "I'll check the horses at six and again at nine. You guys take midnight and four a.m. My phone will be on if you have any problems."

"Okay, boss," Ben said, running his fingers through his hair. "I sure hope it's not too violent."

"Me too. Be careful comin' and goin', and if it gets crazy stay here in the barn or come up to the house. I'll leave the door unlocked in case. Don't hesitate."

"We won't, believe me," Jeb declared. "That damn Devil Wind is no fun."

Saying their goodbyes, Ben and Jeb left through the door at the end of the barn, while Beau and Nickie walked through the tack room and into the yard.

"It sounds serious, Beau," Nickie remarked as they made their way to the house.

"It is," he said solemnly, as the wind suddenly made itself known with a strong gust.

"I assume this is how The Devil Wind starts," she mumbled, staring up at the waving trees as Ben had earlier.

"Yep. Up at Flat Top Point you'd be beggin' for cover already. In a couple of hours or so it'll be blowin' pretty hard down here, but when the sun sets it really gets to whippin' things around, and it just keeps gettin' worse overnight."

"I'm glad I'll be here with you," she remarked, looping her arm through his. "It sounds like an endless tornado."

"It kinda is. A twister with no twist! I'm gonna remember that."

Entering through the kitchen door, they found the table set for three, and a delicious aroma wafting through the air.

"I thought we should have a hearty meal," Gina declared, walking in from the pantry. "I made vegetarian lasagne. That should get us through. I didn't know if you eat meat, Nickie. So many people don't these days."

"I do on occasion, but I haven't had lasagne in ages. It sounds wonderful, thank you."

"I need to start shutterin' the windows," Beau declared. "Shouldn't take more than half-an-hour."

"Beau, before I forget," Gina began, "you got a message earlier. A man named Joseph Pantera called. He said he's staying at the Hollister and to call him back."

"What the f—?" Nickie exclaimed, catching herself before saying the forbidden word. "Beau! Why don't you look surprised?"

"I knew a J. Pantera was comin' in," he admitted, "but I didn't know if that would be your father or brother."

"Why didn't you tell me?"

"Would you have had a fun day if I had? You were gonna know soon enough, and now you do. I'll call him from my study."

"Wait! Don't. All he's going to do is—"

"You don't know what he wants, and after I talk to him I'll tell you everything," he said calmly, then placing his hands on her shoulders, he added, "Nickie, we've gotta face this thing head on."

"That almost got you killed with Gerald."

"I don't think your dad is gonna pick up a lead pipe and come after me. Sit down and catch your breath. I'll be right back."

"Does someone want to tell me what's going on?" Gina piped up. "It may not be any of my business, but when you start talking about murder and lead pipes I think I need to know."

"Fill her in, Nickie. It'll give you something to do while I call your father."

"I'm coming with you."

"No, you're not," he said sternly. "You're gonna sit your butt down and tell Gina what's been goin' on."

"Why would you tell your maid about your personal life," Nickie whispered. "I mean, I get that you like her and everything but—?

"Nickie!"

"Okay, okay, I'm sorry."

"I'll make us some fresh coffee," Gina offered as Beau strode from the room. "You can tell me your story. Maybe I'll be able to help."

"Okay, and, uh, I didn't mean to offend you. Things are different here."

"I've got pretty thick skin," Gina said with a wink. "Sit down and start talking while I get out the mugs."

\* \* \*

Entering his study and closing the door behind him, Beau settled at his desk, took a breath, then called the hotel, but he asked to speak with Amy.

"This is Amy Shepherd."

"Hi, Amy. It's Beau."

"Beau? Oh, hi. This is a surprise. What's up?"

"The bigwig in the Holmby Suite, is he travelin' alone?"

"No. He arrived in a big Mercedes driven by a chauffeur. The chauffeur is in a different room."

"Have you seen Gerald Harris? That was the guy drivin' the black Mercedes who checked out early this mornin'.""

"Not since he left. He was weird. He had a scowl on his face every time I saw him."

"Thanks, hon. Put me back to the switchboard, please."

"Sure, hold on."

Feeling somewhat reassured, he waited while the operator connected him to Joseph Pantera, but the man that answered took him by surprise. Beau had expected Joseph Pantera's voice to be heavy and deep, but it sounded like that of an elderly man.

"Mr. Pantera, Beau Chapman returning your call."

"Thank you. May I call you Beau?"

"Sure," Beau replied, taken aback a second time by the man's unexpected request.

"I would prefer that we speak in person. Would you be so kind as to swing by the hotel? I'm sure you know it. Perhaps we could break bread. I'm eager to try the restaurant here. I've been told they have locally caught fish."

"When would you like to do this?" Beau asked, wondering why the man wanted to speak with him face to face.

"Perhaps in about an hour? I'm tied up for a while, but let's say four o'clock, if that would be convenient."

"That would be fine, but I won't be able to stay long. There's a windstorm comin' in, and it starts to get real bad when the sun begins to set."

"I just heard about this. I'm sure an hour will be plenty of time."

"Then I'll see you in the restaurant at four."

Ending the call, Beau pondered the man's attitude and voice. He'd been extremely polite, but that didn't mean he wasn't tough. A business didn't become as successful as Pantera Jeans without a strong man at the helm.

"I sure am curious," he muttered. "Why the heck do you wanna talk to me?"

The nasty incident with Gerald couldn't be ignored, and deciding on an ounce of prevention, Beau picked up the phone and called Tyler.

"Hey, Beau. Ready for the Devil Wind?"

"Yep. All the horses are in the barn with the shutters bolted. Tyler, what time is your shift over?"

"Around four. Why?"

"Nickie's father arrived in town, and that's right when I'll be meetin' him at the Hollister. I'm not happy about leavin' her by herself. The boys are in their cabin, and Gina's here, but—"

"Say no more. George and I will come by when we log out. We'll probably get there about ten after."

"I'll make sure she and Gina have your number, but as long as I know you'll be there shortly after I leave, that's great."

"If I can get us there earlier I will."

"Thanks, Tyler. I'll let them know you'll be arrivin'. Speak to you later."

"Yep. Stay safe."

"You too. Bye."

"Bye, Beau."

As he hung up the phone, a sudden howling gust caught his attention. He grimaced. They were in for a wild night. Knowing Nickie would be waiting anxiously for the news, he hurried back to the kitchen.

"It was no big deal, Nickie," he declared, walking in. "Your dad was real nice. I'm meetin' up with him in an hour."

"You are? Why? Are you sure that's a good idea?"

"The best way to find out what's on a man's mind is by talkin' to him," he replied, grabbing a jacket from the coat rack. "Tyler and George will be comin' over after their shift, so you'll only be by yourselves for a short time. I'm off to get the shutters closed up. Won't be long."

"You know," Gina said kindly, seeing the worry on Nickie's face, "your dad is doing what all dads do."

"What do you mean?"

"Rich or poor, all fathers want to keep their children safe and happy, and the thing is, Nickie, Gerald could have told him a whopper of a story."

"Oh, my gosh. I hadn't thought about that, and dad would've listened. He likes Gerald. Shit. Gerald must have said something. How else would dad even know about Beau? But as far as Gerald knows, Beau's just my new contractor."

"Uh, Nickie, anyone seeing the two of you together...well...it's obvious you're crazy about each other, but even if Gerald's not that switched on, he's a jealous, possessive jerk. He would have assumed something was going on."

"You're right!"

"It's possible your father just wants to meet Beau to discuss the house, but you'll find out soon enough," Gina said pointedly, then pausing, she asked, "Why do you think he likes Gerald?"

"He pushed me into marrying him," Nickie muttered with a frown, "and then he tried to talk me into staying with him. I think that's proof enough."

"Your father probably supported the marriage because he's old-fashioned. He didn't know how it came about, right?"

"Of course not. I wasn't about to tell him Gerald had been nothing but a drunken one-night stand."

"Exactly, so he gave you his blessing and wanted to support you through what he assumed was a rough patch. He probably thought you were over-reacting wanting a divorce so quickly. I have a feeling you can be that way. Am I right?"

"Well, yeah, kind of. I just wish I could be at that dinner. My father and Beau, good grief."

"Trust Beau, and give your father the benefit of the doubt. He might surprise you."

"I can see why Beau likes you so much."

"Thanks, Nickie, I appreciate that. You want some more coffee?"

"I want that lasagne, I wish he'd hurry up, but sure, I'll take some more coffee while we wait."

As Gina rose from the table to fetch the coffee pot, Nickie stared out the window just as Beau was closing the shutters. Catching her eye, he sent her a wave.

"Even if you and dad have a meeting of the minds, there's still Gerald to worry about," she murmured, as the shutter closed, "and I know him. He's not going to walk away quietly."

## CHAPTER NINETEEN

Though Beau wanted to devour the delicious lasagne sitting in front of him, he allowed himself only a small serving. He didn't want to sit down at a dinner table with Nickie's father and order only coffee.

"Gina, it's fabulous," Nickie declared. "I wish I could cook."

"If you're around a while I could teach you a thing or two, but it's like anything. To be good at something you have to enjoy it."

"All I've never done is make toast, and I like doing that," Nickie said with a laugh. "Wow! Listen to that wind. I wish I could see out the windows."

"This is nothing," Gina remarked. "Give it a couple of hours and believe me, you'll be glad the shutters are up."

"Gina, I think you should stay over," Beau said solemnly. "I'll worry if you're at your house by yourself."

"You don't have to twist my arm. I'd much prefer to be here."

"Damn, look at the time," Beau said, glancing at his watch. "I've gotta shower and change."

As he pushed back from the table and moved quickly from the room, Nickie leaned back in her chair and let out a groan.

"I wish I knew why dad came all the way here and didn't call me first. Maybe I should go after Beau leaves and surprise them, or at least call the hotel and speak to him. I need to find out what the hell is going on."

"Nickie, I really advise you to let Beau handle this."

"Easier said than done."

"Have some more lasagne and wine. It'll calm your nerves."

"Gina, can I ask you something?"

"Sure," Gina replied, ladling the second helping onto Nickie's plate.

"I don't mean to be rude or anything, but you and Beau, you're so close, but you're his maid. I don't understand."

"Maid?" Gina exclaimed, then to Nickie's surprise, she began to laugh.

"What did I say?"

"I've never thought of myself as his maid, but I suppose I am. I used to own this ranch. Beau bought it off me a few years back."

"He did?"

"He worked here during the summer during his college years, and let me tell you, from the moment he arrived we knew he had a rare gift. Ralph, my husband, would be having trouble with a difficult horse, and Beau would walk up, quietly take the lead rope from Ralph's hand, and in a few minutes that horse would be like butter, all soft and sweet."

"You're kidding?"

"Nope. Beau just has a way about him. His dad is a big-time homebuilder in Dallas and that's where Beau learned about construction, but Beau's heart is in horses."

"How did he end up buying this ranch?"

"Well," Gina began, dropping her eyes to the table, "Ralph got sick. By that time Beau was working in his father's company, but he came down to help out and stayed in the cabin with the other ranch hand. It wasn't long before he took over the training program. Ralph could stand at the fence and advise, but he was too weak to ride. Then one day he went into the hospital, and never came out."

"Gina, that's so sad. I'm sorry."

"Those were difficult days, and Beau became my rock. He kept the place running, but it wasn't long before I realized I needed to sell. It was only natural Beau should be the new owner. It took some doing on his part, financially I mean, but it all worked out. I opened my bakery, something I'd always wanted to do, and that's that."

"So, why do you do all his housework and stuff?"

"Starting business kept me busy, but the transition was tough. I was lonely, and I missed the horses and the ranch. One morning I stopped by to say hello. I popped my head in the door, and I was shocked. What a mess. Beau was so busy with clients and horses and all the work a ranch needs, the house was bottom on the list. I had nowhere to be, so I went to work. I started the laundry, and as I was cleaning up the kitchen I found myself humming. That's when it hit me. Without a man in my life to take care of I felt lost. He was thrilled. I would gladly do this for nothing, but he insists on paying me."

"That's quite a story. No wonder you and Beau are so close."

"You talkin' about me?" Beau asked as he walked in.

"My gosh, look at you!" Nickie exclaimed, taking in the slacks, crisp white shirt and sports coat. "You could be on the cover of GQ!"

"I thought I should make an effort. I'm glad you approve."

"Approve, are you kidding?  You have to take me out one night dressed like that."

"You've got a deal," he promised, kissing her lightly. "I'll call you when I'm leavin', but I'm takin' Betsy so it'll be quick. She doesn't have bluetooth."

"Why aren't you taking the jeep?"

"The truck is safer in this wind. She's heavier for one thing, and the window glass is thicker and stronger."

"The wind is that bad?"

"Not yet, but there'll be debris flyin' around. Okay, I'm outta here. Tyler and George will be here shortly."

"I still wish you weren't going," she said softly, rising from the table to give him a hug. "Dad is a very busy man. He must be really upset to send Gerald and then come down himself."

"We know nothin'," he said firmly. "Remember that sayin'? To assume makes an ass outta you and me. I'll call as soon as I can."

Quickly kissing her again, he headed out the door.

"I'm sure this will be fine," Gina said reassuringly.

"I hope so," Nickie replied with a sigh. "I don't like the shutters being closed. It makes me nervous. I want to see outside."

"They need to be in place. These winds are bad, but this time tomorrow they'll be gone."

"What about Trixie and the other horses? There's no-one in the barn watching over them."

"My goodness, you really are a worrier. They're used to the elements. I'm sure they're fine."

"Well, I'm not, and I can't just sit around here while Beau is off with my dad. I have to do something. I'm going over there."

Jumping from the table, she marched to the hall closet and grabbed one of Beau's jackets.

"Are you crazy? It's blowing hard out there."

"I'm only walking across the yard," Nickie argued already on her way to the front door. "When Tyler and George show up I'll come back."

"Wait! I'm coming with you."

"Great. You can help me feed them all carrots," Nickie said with a smile, but pushing the open door, she was shocked by the intensity of the gale. "Holy crap! I can't believe this," she exclaimed, hastily closing it.

"I told you," Gina said, pulling on her coat as she walked over to join her. "Are you sure you want to do this?"

"Very sure," Nickie declared. "It just took me by surprise, that's all, but you don't have to come."

"Yes, I do."

"Okay! Are you ready?"

"As I'll ever be."

Battling through the door and making sure it was locked before they left, they ran through the gusts across the yard to the tack room. Lifting the bar from over the front of the door, they stumbled inside, hurriedly closing it behind them.

"It came up so fast," Nickie said breathlessly. "I mean, an hour ago it was just a strong breeze."

"That's how it happens," Gina panted, "and it will get even worse."

"I'm glad we're here. I'll feel so much better once I've checked Trixie. Let's get the carrots."

Each grabbing a handful and starting down the aisle, they were greeted by a chorus of happy nickering, but Nickie abruptly paused.

"Gina? Did you hear that? It sounded like a car."

"I'm not sure, but if you're right it's probably Tyler."

"Oh, of course," Nickie declared, walking into a stall and peering through a crack in the wood. "Oh, no. Gina!"

"What is it?" Gina asked urgently.

"Gerald," Nickie gasped, turning to face her, "and he's with two other guys. This whole thing was a setup. My dad lured Beau away so I'd be here alone."

"Calm down, you don't know any of that," Gina said steadily, "besides, Tyler and George will be here any minute."

"We don't know that either," Nickie protested, her voice rising. "What if Gerald's managed to, I don't know, stop them from getting here somehow? Even if they do arrive, then what?"

"Nickie, you need to calm down. Call Beau, and if you can't reach him, call Tyler."

"Fuck! I don't have my phone. I left it on the kitchen table."

"What? And mine's in my bag."

"Gina, I'm really worried about Beau. It's too weird that Gerald should show up right after he left. I'm not waiting here, no fucking way, and you shouldn't either."

"Nickie, you're overreacting. Beau's in a restaurant at the hotel. I'm sure he's fine, and as for Gerald—"

"You didn't see him pick up a piece of lead pipe to bash Beau's brains in," Nickie interrupted, her voice almost hysterical.

Jerking her eyes back to the narrow slit, she saw Gerald banging on the front door, while his two goons were skirting the house.

"Gina!" she exclaimed, spinning around. "My car. It's behind the barn."

"Where will you go? I honestly think we're safer staying in this barn."

"You can stay if you want, but I'm leaving."

Panic seizing her, she darted out of the stall and began to run down the barn aisle.

"Nickie, wait, I'm not letting you go alone," Gina yelled, chasing after her, but as she passed the tack room she paused. Frantically looking around, she saw what she wanted.

Nickie had reached the regular door next to the large sliding one that opened up the barn. She was about to pull back the bolt when Gina caught up.

"Here, put this on," she panted, trying to catch her breath.

"A riding helmet? But we'll be in the car."

"For one thing, it'll keep your hair from blowing in your eyes when we step out of here, and for another, it could save your life if a flying tree limb whacks you in the head, or smashes through the windshield.

Stop being so damn difficult and do it."

"Oh, yeah. Okay," she replied sheepishly.

Gina quickly donned hers, while Nickie held her hair up with one hand, pulled on the helmet with the other, then buckled the strap under her chin.

"Thanks, Gina. Now let's go before they come over here."

Sliding back the bolt and pushing the door against wind, she slipped outside, then held it open for Gina. The Lexus was just a few feet away, and fighting to get the doors open, they managed to climb inside.

"Obviously we can't drive out on to the street," Nickie muttered. "We'd pass them on the way out. We need to drive someplace they won't be able to see the car. Ah! I know exactly where to go!"

Retrieving the key from under the seat, she started the car and rolled it forward, turning away from the barn and following the dirt track that would take them up to Flat Top Point.

"Nickie, you're not going to the top of the hill, are you? You can't. Drive across the field to the cabin."

"Bad idea. The field is open. He'll recognize my SUV right away."

"Nickie, you don't understand. We'll be blown over if we go up to that flat pad."

"You don't know Gerald. I'd rather be blown over than taken away by that asshole. Besides, this is a big SUV. We'll be fine."

"We won't be fine. This is madness!"

* * *

Outside their cabin, Ben and Jeb were nailing down a loose shutter, Jeb holding it in place while Ben hammered in the nail. Finally getting the job done, they were making their way back inside when Jeb saw a flash of white. Shielding his eyes he looked across the fields and saw the white Lexus climbing the gently sloped hill.

# CHAPTER TWENTY

Walking through the upmarket restaurant at the Hollister Hotel, Beau spotted an attractive, mature man seated alone in a booth perusing a menu.

"Excuse me," he said, approaching the table, "are you Joseph Pantera?"

"I am," the man replied, standing up and extending his hand. "Beau Chapman, I presume."

"It's very good to meet you, Sir," Beau said, surprised the man was so slight of build. "The hostess wasn't at the podium, but I thought I'd be able to find you."

"I would have done the same, and please, call me Joe. Have a seat. I appreciate you venturing out on this dreadful day. I was told the wind would be bad, but when I looked out the window I was truly astonished. It came up so quickly."

"Yes, it does, but I'm used to it," Beau remarked, "and your call has me curious."

"Obviously you know I'm Nicole Harris's father."

"Yes. Nicole has mentioned you, and I know she works for Pantera jeans."

"Before she left, Nicole told me it was Helen Meyer who had found a local contractor, and Helen was kind enough to give me your contact information. I understand you'll be finishing the house. Is that right?"

"That's right. Nicole and I have come to an arrangement, but you say you found me through Helen?"

"That surprises you?"

"It does. When I told Nicole I was meetin' you she thought Gerald had brought you to town."

"Gerald? Nicole's husband? No. I've haven't spoken to him, but

Nicole knows I'm here?"

"She does. She wanted to come with me, but I figured if you'd wanted her to join us you would have asked her."

"Quite right, but how did you keep her away? She can be very determined."

"Uh, I have discovered that," Beau replied, keeping a poker face, but still confused he added, "So, Gerald hasn't been in touch with you?"

"No, I haven't heard from him, but why do you ask? Do you know him?"

"I can't say I know him, and I think I just derailed this conversation. You wanted to know about the house."

"Ah, yes, back to the point. Nicole has had problems building this vacation home of hers. I confess I did promise to stay out of it, and it's her money, but I don't like to see it being wasted. As much as I want to respect her wishes, I've decided to step in. She's probably mad as heck that I'm here, and I'll try not to interfere too much, but I need to see the site, take a look at the plans, and get a feel for what's going on. I'll back out when I feel confident things are moving in the right direction, but I simply will not allow her to flounder any longer."

Try as he might, Beau couldn't conceal his relief—or his shock. Nickie's father was a genial, caring man, who only wanted to make sure his daughter wasn't throwing good money after bad.

"Beau, you look perplexed."

"I, uh, I'm not sure what to say. There's nothin' else you want to talk to me about?"

"What else could there be? Mind you, I was going to warn you. Nicole isn't the easiest woman to work for. I want to see this project finished, and I'd like to offer my help if you hit any rough spots, because," he said, pausing dramatically, "dealing with Nicole, you will."

"I have experienced Nicole's temperament," Beau remarked, inwardly smiling as he thought about Nickie's bottom a deep shade of pink from his spanking. "I think I have a handle on it, but just to be clear, you said you didn't know Nicole's husband was here?"

"No. Nicole didn't tell me he was coming to join her. I know he's out of town, but I was under the impression he was off on one of his golfing jaunts."

"This is awkward," Beau said slowly. "I'm not even sure..."

"I think," Joe said, fixing him with a steady gaze, "we should have a glass of wine, order some of that local fish, then I'd like to hear what else is going on."

"Joe, that is an excellent suggestion. There's quite a bit to—" but the chiming of his phone cut him off. "I'm sorry, please excuse me. This might be important."

Pulling the phone from his pocket, he stared at the screen. It was a text from Jeb.

**Just saw Nickie's Lexus climbing the hill to Flat Top Point.**

"What the hell?"

"Beau? Is something wrong?"

"Something is very wrong and I have to go. Uh, Joe, I think you'd better come with me. I'll explain on the way. You don't mind being in an old truck, do you? It's the safest vehicle you can be in during this wind."

"I don't mind at all."

Moving quickly through the restaurant and out the hotel doors, Beau led him through the blustery wind, but as they approached Betsy, Joe broke into a broad grin. Holding open the door as the gale whipped around them, Joe climbed in, then Beau hurried around and settled behind the wheel.

"This truck," Joe began, "she's a beauty."

"Thanks," Beau said, starting it up. "I restored it myself. Her name's Betsy."

"This is an amazing coincidence. My father had one of these when I was a kid. He started the clothing company, and he'd pile the garments in the back and I'd go with him when he made his deliveries to the local stores. This is incredible."

"I'm glad you like it, but we've got a big problem," Beau said urgently, rolling from the hotel grounds. "I don't mean to scare you, but Nickie is doin' something reckless. I need to get to her, but while we're drivin' I'll tell you what's been goin' on."

As Beau was leaving the hotel, Tyler and George were turning into the driveway at Beau's ranch. With the wind swirling leaves, twigs and dust through the air, they were shocked to see Gerald Harris trying to remove one of the shutters from a front window, and two other men skulking around the side of the house.

"I'll handle this," George growled, stepping from the car and out into the wild weather.

Calling for backup, Tyler watched his powerfully built partner march through the howling winds. Though they'd been together for years, Tyler was still amazed at the sheer size and strength of the man.

"Hey!" George called, his voice booming through the bluster.

Assuming it was Beau, Gerald reached into his waistband and pulled out a short, hard club, but as he turned around and saw the huge man ambling towards him, he staggered backwards and fell against the house.

"I, uh, I, just came by to apologize to Beau," Gerald yelled. "He, uh, didn't answer the door, and I was worried maybe something had happened."

Tyler watched, almost chuckling, as George lumbered forward, grabbed Gerald by the elbow, and hauled him back to the Mercedes like a father dragging his naughty child. In spite of the severe winds, George was able to open the car door and throw him in the back seat, then climbing behind the wheel, he picked up the key sitting in its small compartment in the center console.

Looking back at the house, George squinted as he sought out the two accomplices. They were trying to run, but they had no hope of winning against the powerful gusts. Warning Gerald to stay put, George soon had them corralled, and he'd just put them in the car with Gerald when Beau's truck came racing up the driveway.

* * *

Seeing Tyler's car, then the Mercedes with big George standing next to it, rather than fight the wind to get answers, he grabbed his phone.

"What the heck's goin' on?" he asked the moment Tyler answered.

"Sure am glad you're here," Tyler replied. "We just arrived and found Harris and two goons trying to break into your house. George rounded them up and put them in the Mercedes. I've called for back up. The boys should be here any minute."

"You won't believe this," Beau said urgently. "Jeb texted me. He saw the Lexus headed up to Flat Top Point. It must be Nickie!"

"Dammit!" Tyler exclaimed. "How did she get to her car?"

"It was parked behind the barn. She must've been checkin' the horses. I'll bet she saw Gerald drive up and panicked. Her father is with me. I'm gonna drive into the garage and let him into the house, then go after her. Ask George to meet me there."

"Just like her mother," Joe muttered.

"Her mother is a reckless, overreactin', stubborn princess too? Sorry, Joe," Beau said hastily as he continued down the driveway. "I'm just worried sick. Nickie's drivin' to a real dangerous place and I've gotta stop her."

"No need to apologize. I love her very much, but you just described my wife."

"Why is Gerald so hell bent on gettin' Nickie home?" Beau said angrily. "It's obvious she can't stand the guy."

"Ah, yes, that would be my fault."

"Your fault?"

"When Gerald married her I made him sign many pieces of paper. One of them stipulated if either of them filed for divorce within the first year, Gerald wouldn't be entitled to anything. In two years there was a small amount, and so on. I did it in the hope it would help him be patient with her."

"That explains a few things," Beau grimaced as he swung into the garage. "I assume the year is up soon?"

"In a couple of weeks."

"Looks like you and Nickie have a lot to talk about."

"I had no idea she was so unhappy," Joe said with a sigh. "Please, Beau, bring her home safely, and by the way, I've always called her Nickie too."

"Really? Thanks for tellin' me, and you bet I will. Excuse me, I have to talk to George real quick."

Jumping from the truck, Beau hurried to the large man and explained what he needed, then opened the door that led into the house.

"Please, Joe, make yourself at home," he said, showing him inside. "Tyler will be here shortly. He's gettin' Gerald and his guys transported."

"I certainly didn't expect such drama when I drove into this sleepy town," Joe said shaking his head. "I can't thank you enough for explaining everything, and watching out for my daughter."

"There's more, but I have to go. George? Are you ready?"

"I'm good," the big man called.

"Wish me luck," Beau said, heading back to the truck.

"My luck and my prayers," Joe murmured. "All that I can muster."

## CHAPTER TWENTY-ONE

Things were not boding well for Nickie and Gina. They were almost at the top of the slope, but to Nickie's horror the winds had grown fierce and were quaking the car.

Afraid to distract Nickie from her driving, Gina had clung with a white knuckle grip to the seat belt during the terrifying climb, but she knew the hell waiting if Nickie continued.

"Nicky, you absolutely cannot drive onto the flat pad," she yelled frantically. "Don't you understand? We'll be flipped over. You have to find a way to turn around."

"There is nowhere, and I can't back all the way down the fucking hill."

A savage gust suddenly hit the car, rocking it wildly. Screaming, Nickie hit the brakes and dropped her head to the steering wheel.

"Oh, my, God. You were right. I should never have come up here."

"Nickie, just back down. You can do it. You can."

"How much worse could it be?" Nickie muttered, lifting her eyes to the top of the slope. "It's no distance. I'll only go in enough to turn around, and I'll go really fast."

Before Gina could shout another protest, Nickie gunned the engine, shooting the car up and over the crest of the hill.

She'd made a terrible mistake.

Copious amounts of debris were flying through the air and began slamming against the car. Panic-stricken she turned the wheel, but she was too late. The powerful wind began sliding them sideways.

"We have to get out, we have to get out," Gina screamed. "Get out and crawl back to the road."

"Crawl back to the road? Are you insane?" Nickie wailed, but when another gust threatened to tip the car over, she stared at Gina in horror.

"Fuck! Tell me what to do!"

"Get out of the car, but don't hold on to the door. The wind will rip it away from you. Just let it go and fall on your stomach. Keep your face to the ground and crawl as fast as you can back towards the road, but we need to do this at the same time."

"Gina, I'm so scared, I'm so fucking scared."

"I know, I am too, but we have to do this right now. Ready?"

"No, but—"

"On three!" Gina shouted "One, two, three."

As Gina had warned, the moment Nickie opened her door it was instantly wrenched from her grip. Throwing herself to the ground, panting and sobbing, she scrabbled forward not even sure which direction she was headed. Lifting her gaze to get her bearings, the car rocked beside her issuing strange sounds, its doors flailing like a bizarre steel creature in pain. Feverishly crawling around the back, she peered down the passenger side in search of Gina.

Nickie's blood ran cold.

Gina was on her back lying completely still, the passenger door swinging inches from her head.

"Gina!"

Though she had shrieked the name, Nickie knew her voice had been lost in the tumultuous gale. Trying to control her terror she slithered forward on her stomach. Though Beau's thick coat offered some protection, objects were hitting her body and legs, sometimes painfully, and her face was stinging. Her heart pounding wildly, she finally reached Gina. In spite of her helmet, a nasty gash oozed blood above the bridge of her nose.

"Gina, oh, no, this is all my fault," Nickie sobbed. "I'm so sorry. Please, wake up. Please."

Letting out a low, deep groan, Gina rolled her head to the side.

"Thank, God, thank, God," Nickie blubbered, but an ominous creak snapped her back to the life-threatening danger. "I have to move you. Don't worry, I can do this, I can."

Clenching her teeth, with the wind and debris raging around her, she put her hands underneath Gina's arms. Wriggling her way backwards, pulling her with all her might, inch by inch, her eyes shut tight to protect them from the stinging dust, she managed to slide Gina away from the car.

Breathless and weak, she looked around to find the road, but was met with a sight that shook her to the core. The car had swung around, and the passenger door was hanging at a bizarre angle. They'd been minutes, possibly seconds, from death.

Completely mortified and on the verge of hysteria, Nickie used her last ounce of strength to roll Gina on her stomach to protect her face from further injury, then collapsed next to her, burying her head in her arms. The fury raging over her head sounded like a gigantic demon breathing its mayhem upon the earth.

"The Devil Wind," she muttered, and as her lips tasted dirt, she began to pray.

*Dear Lord. I'm sorry I never pray, and I'm sorry for all those times I went to church and never paid attention. I always hear life is a precious gift, but I didn't really know what that meant until now. I'm going to have horses, and not just for me, but horses that I can help, and I'm going to make up with mom, and tell my dad how much I love him. And Beau, I've fallen in love for the first time, and I'm going to tell him. Please, dear God, please let me get out of here, and please help Gina, please.*

For a miraculous moment, the fury seemed to abate. Daring to risk a peek over her arm, she raised her head. Though she barely had any breath left in her, she gasped. The Lexus was on its side and half way across the pad, but that wasn't the only thing that made her catch her breath.

Everything was shrouded in a strange, dim glow, as if The Devil Wind really was a huge demon casting its evil shadow across the earth.

A chill pricked her skin.

Shifting her eyes from the car, she looked across to the mountains in the distance. The odd scene was caused by the fading light. Night was falling.

Fresh sobs racked her body as she dropped her face back down. No-one knew they were there. It was the last place anyone would even think to look. Reaching out her arm, she wrapped it around Gina's waist.

"If we're going to die, at least we won't die alone."

* * *

The Devil Wind called her name.

Had she been lying in the dirt five minutes or an hour?

The mocking wail happened again.

"Nicki..."

But it was clearer.

"Nickie..."

*It was human!*

Almost afraid to believe help had arrived, she gingerly lifted her eyes and peered into the howling gloom. There was nothing to see.

"Nickie..."

The deep bellow came from behind her. Eyes scrunched, she looked over her shoulder. Like a great lion, George was crawling towards her. A wave of relieved tears cascaded down her face, and she gestured he should go to Gina first. Cupping her hand around her forehead to protect her eyes, she watched him roll Gina over, study her face, then struggle with a sleeping bag, zipping her inside it as he shimmied it up her body. Uncoiling a rope from his waist, he wrapped it around her, tying her up like a parcel.

It was only then Nickie saw the rope trailing out behind him, flapping in the wind. To her amazement, he pulled out a cellphone, touched the screen, and moments later the rope grew taut. The sleeping bag, with Gina tucked safely inside, began to slide slowly across the ground.

"Keep your head down!" he yelled, then turning around, still on his hands and knees, he followed Gina.

Nickie buried her head back into the crook of her arm. Though she knew he'd be back for her, she wasn't sure she'd survive. Even when he returned and began cocooning her inside the sleeping bag, she was sure a piece of flying bark would slice her in two. As the rope tightened around her and she began sliding across the grass, she thought the tether would snap and she'd be sucked up by The Devil Wind and thrown over the cliff. But when she felt herself being lifted up, she dared to look. Beau's smoky-blue eyes stared down at her.

Moments later she was inside the truck and he was unwrapping her. George was next to her with Gina curled in his lap, the sleeping bag loose around her shoulders. As Beau began the slow drive down the dirt track, Nickie closed her eyes and let the tears flow. She'd been plucked from the jaws of hell and was on her way home.

Two ambulances were waiting, and as Gina was loaded into one, Nickie protested vehemently.

"Please, I hate hospitals. Just let me lie down inside. Please. I'm okay."

Not wanting to argue, Beau swept her up and he carried her into the house. Laying her on the bed in the guest room, the paramedic checked her over.

"You are one lucky lady," he declared as he treated the many scrapes on her hands and face. "You seem to be okay, but don't hesitate to come into emergency if you start having dizzy spells or other problems."

"Thank you," she managed. "What about Gina?"

"She was awake and talking, but she was taken to emergency to be on the safe side. She might have a concussion."

As Beau walked him out, Nickie's father settled on the edge of the bed.

"I'm so glad you're here," she stammered, fresh tears springing from her eyes. "But I don't understand? Why did you come, and what happened to Gerald?"

"Gerald's behind bars, and I didn't send him here," her father said softly, gently taking her hand.

"You didn't?"

"No, and we'll discuss all that later. Right now you need to rest and heal," he said, his voice cracking. "My precious little girl. I'm so glad you're all right."

"Dad, I can't stop shaking."

"I'm not surprised," Beau remarked as he walked back in. "You're exhausted and traumatized. You need a hot bath if you're up to it, then sleep."

"A bath? Oh, yes, I'd love that."

"The paramedics have left you a sedative. You'll take that when you're in bed so you can get the rest you need."

"Beau's right," her father said with a sigh. "You've been through an incredible ordeal. We can talk tomorrow when you're feeling better."

"Beau, I'm so sorry."

"Hush. Come with me. It's time for a soak in Epsom salts. I'll get the water runnin'."

"No need," Tyler announced, poking his head through the door. "The tub's ready and waiting."

"Thanks, Tyler," Beau said gratefully. "Okay, Nickie, let's get you upstairs."

"Everything's going to be fine," her father said, kissing her on the forehead as she rose unsteadily from the bed. "I'll be right here if you need anything."

Sweeping her up, Beau carried her up the stairs and into his bedroom. As he stood her on her feet and peeled off her clothes, he discovered bruises in odd spots across her body.

"You poor thing," he mumbled, walking her into the bathroom. "Get in slowly."

"This feels so good," she murmured, sinking into the hot water. "Ouch. I hurt everywhere."

"I'm sure you do. Listen, I hate to leave you, but I've gotta get to the hospital. I'm the closest thing to family Gina has."

"Oh, yes, of course. I understand. She was knocked out. It might be serious."

"When you're done, get into bed. I'll leave the sleepin' pill and a glass of water on the nightstand, and I'll have my phone with me if you need anything. I promise I won't be long."

"My phone," she frowned. "I left it on the kitchen table. That's why I couldn't call you from the barn."

"I wanna hear all about that, but it can wait until tomorrow. There's a regular phone on the nightstand."

"Okay. Uh, Beau, before you go there's something very important I need to tell you. Maybe I shouldn't say this, but if you left and something happened..."

"Hey, nothin's gonna happen."

"I don't know that," she muttered. "The Devil Wind is still blowing, and I have to say this."

"Okay, I'm listenin', sweetheart," he said, sitting on the edge of the tub. "Go ahead."

"If you never want to see me again I'll understand. I'm a complete idiot," she mumbled, the tears flowing down her face, "but I love you with my whole heart. I thought I was going to die, and the only thing I could think about was telling you that, because it's true. I've never felt like this in my life, not about anything or anyone. There, I've said it. You don't have to say anything back, it's—"

Filled with his own fervent need to show her how he felt, his lips suddenly fell on hers in a warm, gentle, loving kiss.

"I'm crazy in love with you too," he murmured, breaking away. "When I discovered you were on your way up to Flat Top my dang heart stopped. I knew at that moment I couldn't bear it if anything happened to you."

"Beau..."

"You soak and go to bed. I'll be back soon."

As he left the bathroom, she leaned back and closed her eyes. There wasn't any part of her that didn't hurt, but she was alive.

* * *

Anxious to get to the hospital, Beau said a hurried goodbye to Tyler, George and Joseph, then hurried to the garage and climbed into his truck.

But the drive to the hospital was perilous.

Tree limbs were scattered everywhere and power lines were down, but with the streets deserted he was able to maneuver around them. Parking close to the entrance, he pushed through the wind into emergency, and was directed to Gina's room. Though they were keeping her overnight, to his great relief her wounds were superficial. She'd received a few stitches and been given a sedative, but had suffered no concussion. Sitting at her bedside, he didn't want to leave until she fell asleep.

"That sedative is knocking me out," she murmured, "and my head is killing me, but Beau, there's something you need to know about Nickie."

He took a breath and prepared himself. There wasn't much he'd be able to offer in her defense. What was done was done, and if Gina never wanted to lay eyes on the reckless girl again he couldn't blame her.

"What she did," Gina slowly began, "was impulsive, and she refused to listen to reason, but she did something else, something amazing. To be honest I barely remember it, but in that pummeling Devil Wind, she dragged me away from the car. It could have flipped over at any time, and I vaguely remember the door swinging right next to my head. Beau, I don't know how she managed it, but Nickie risked her life to save me."

"She did?"

"She's got heart, Beau, she's got heart and she's got incredible courage."

"Thank you for tellin' me," he muttered, trying to process the remarkable news, "but you need to rest now. Close your eyes and go to sleep."

"I can't keep them open."

"I love you, Gina. I'll pick you up when you're ready to go home. Whatever you need, just let me know."

"I love you too."

He sat for a moment, watching her drift away and thinking about what she'd told him, then walking quietly from her room, he closed the door behind him and headed back into the wild night. The drive home was just as hair-raising. Finally turning into his driveway, he noticed Tyler's car was gone. Gratefully rolling into his garage, relieved the drama was at an end, he let out a deep breath, then climbed from the truck and walked into the kitchen. Joseph sat at the table nursing a drink.

"How's your friend?" Joe asked. "Nothing serious, I hope."

"She'll be fine, thank goodness. They're keepin' her overnight, and I'm glad. Drivin' out there is nuts. Goes without sayin' the guest room is yours. Not as nice as your hotel suite, but you're most welcome."

"Thank you. I'm very grateful. I want to be here when Nickie wakes up. I need to know she's okay and how this happened. I have so many questions."

"You and me both, though I can guess the answer to most of them," he remarked, raising his eyebrows. "Make yourself at home. You'll find clean towels in the bathroom. I'd like to sit and chat, but honestly, I'm beat up."

"Of course you are, and I'm ready for bed myself. Thank you for everything, Beau," Joseph said, rising to his feet. "I don't know how I'll be able to repay you for rescuing my little girl."

The two men hugged, then Beau walked slowly up the stairs. As he entered his bedroom, though the bedside lamp was still glowing, he could see Nickie was sound asleep. Moving quietly across to the bed, he sat down softly and stared at the many scratches on her face. Her hair was still damp from the bath, and he was tempted to wipe the stray hairs off her face, but he didn't want to wake her.

"I'm sorry, Nickie, I should have waited until Tyler and George arrived," he murmured. "I'll find a way to make this up to you, I swear."

"Gina?" she whispered, though her eyes remained closed.

"Gina's fine."

"Thank, God...so sorry."

"Sleep darlin'. I'm gonna jump in the shower."

"Love you."

"I love you too."

Leaning down, he touched his lips to a cut on the side of her cheek, then rising to his feet, he made his way wearily into the bathroom. As he stepped into the shower and let the hot water wash over his body, he couldn't help but wonder about the days ahead. Did he have a future with Nickie? She might love him, but life on his ranch was a far cry from her luxury lifestyle.

## CHAPTER TWENTY-TWO
### One Week Later

Though Jospeh Pantera could only stay in town one more day, Beau arranged for him to meet Geoff, the architect, and Daniel from the city, then walked him through Nickie's half-built house. It was littered with debris, but there was no serious damage, and Beau discovered Joe was surprisingly  knowledgeable when it came to construction.

"I'll keep you in the loop as things progress," Beau promised. "You have my word."

"I appreciate it," Joe said gratefully, "and I'll do my best not to step on my daughter's toes."

"You don't have to worry about that," Beau assured him. "If you have an idea I want to hear it, and she will too. I don't think I'll have any problems getting this house finished."

"I believe you," Joe replied with a grin. "I'm not sure why, but I do."

* * *

Following her release from the hospital, Gina stayed at the ranch, and Nickie insisted on taking care of her. Beau helped Ben and Jeb clean up the mess left by the Devil Wind, and firmed up the subcontractors. Two days after Gina had returned to her own home, and life was beginning to return to normal, Beau and Nickie had just finished breakfast when Beau reached across the table for her hand.

"The dust has settled. I'm back workin' with my horses, and my crew will be at your house next week. There are two messes to clean up now. What the last builder left behind, and the Devil Wind, but you're finally gonna see it gettin' built."

"I know, I can't believe it," she said with a happy smile. "I can't wait. Do you really think it will be finished by fall?"

"Maybe before, if we don't hit any snags." Then pausing, he squeezed her hand and leaned across the table. "Nickie, it's time to deal with what happened."

"Uh, you mean, how I took off up to Flat Top?" she asked, the glint in his smoky-blue eyes sending her butterflies bursting to life.

"Yep."

"I explained all that! I didn't have my phone, and I was terrified Gerald would come into the barn."

"But we both know you could've bolted the barn and tack room doors, and if you felt you absolutely had to run, Jeb and Ben were just across the field. You also knew Tyler and George were on their way."

"Not for sure," she protested. "Anything could have happened, and Gerald would have seen me if I'd driven to the cabin."

"You know full well those two boys can handle themselves, but more importantly, didn't I tell you that you were never to go up to Flat Top durin' a heavy wind?"

"Uh, yeah," she said sheepishly, dropping her eyes.

"And I bet Gina did too."

"Uh-huh, but I was so scared," she bleated. "I had to get away."

"You remind me of a hot little mare. You get spooked and bolt. You've gotta learn to take a minute and think things through. You can't keep losin' your temper and bein' impulsive."

"I know," she murmured with a heavy sigh.

"I haven't mentioned this, but Gina told me how you dragged her away from the car," he said, lowering his voice. "That was incredibly brave and I'm real proud of you, but it should never have happened in the first place."

"I know that too."

"I'm takin' you back up to Flat Top."

"You mean..."

"Yep. I'm gonna spank you when we get there."

"Yes, Sir," she murmured, a flush crossing her face.

"I also wanna see how bad it is and where your car ended up. It'll need to be towed out."

"I'm curious about that myself."

"Go on upstairs and change into a skirt and flat shoes, then meet me in the garage."

"Yes, Sir," she repeated, rising from the table.

As she disappeared up the stairs, he cleared the dishes, loaded them in the dishwasher, then headed out to the garage. By the time she returned, he'd stowed the items he needed in the truck and was waiting behind the wheel.

"You don't have any doubt you deserve to be punished, do you?" he asked as she climbed in.

"No, Sir. I shouldn't have gone up there after you warned me, and I should have listened to Gina. There are other things too."

"I just wanted to make sure we're ridin' the same trail."

Though she remained quiet on the drive through the ranch, she began to comment as they started up the slope and the evidence of the tumult began to appear.

"Look at all the branches."

"Believe it or not, Ben and Jeb cleared this."

"They did?"

"You can't imagine what it was like."

"My gosh. Will we be able to make it all the way up?"

"Sure, but I don't know how I made it up and back that night. It was one of the worst Devil Winds I've ever seen. I'm not sure what we're gonna find at the top. Ben said we'd need a couple of tractors."

"Honestly, I'm not surprised," she murmured. "The winds were so fierce, and it lasted for hours and hours."

"Yep, you're right about that."

Approaching the crest he accelerated the last few yards, and as he drove on to the flat pad, Nickie gasped, and Beau let out a low whistle.

"Dang. I have never seen it like this. Isn't that a door off your Lexus?"

"Holy crap. Yeah. That's a door. I can't believe what I'm seeing. It looks like there's been a war here."

"There was. Nature's war."

As he cautiously continued towards the line of trees on the far side, they discovered her car on its side. The mangled metal was wrapped around one of the larger pines.

"If Gina hadn't made you jump out..." he said gravely, stopping the truck as his voice trailed off. "Nickie, do you have any idea how lucky you are to be alive?"

"It's a miracle."

"Yep, and miracles don't happen very often, so I'm gonna make sure we don't need another one any time soon," he said grimly, climbing from the truck, and reaching behind his seat, he retrieved a sleeping bag and a length of rope. "Come on, Nickie."

Stepping out, she followed him a short distance, and though filled with curiosity as he flapped open the bag, she didn't ask any questions.

"Hold this up against the tree, press your body and face against it, then wrap your arms around the trunk."

She gazed at a him, the penny dropping.

"Now, Nickie!"

As she did as he instructed, he tied her wrists together, and with her face to the side, she had an unobstructed view of the pandemonium.

"I'm gonna spank your butt as you look at the chaos," he said sternly. "Bein' punished in the place you and Gina could've lost your lives should make the point very clear. Keep your eyes open, and think about that as I tan your backside."

His words sent her pulse racing, and when she felt him unzip her skirt and tug it down, her fluttering butterflies turned into flapping sparrows. Moments later his fingers slipped into the waistband of her panties, and she cringed as he slid them down her legs.

"Leave them around your ankles, and think about the choices you made. I'll be back shortly."

\* \* \*

Leaning against his truck and studying the carnage, Beau recalled the shards of icy fear that had gripped his heart on that spine-chilling night. Not only had the winds been horrendous, he didn't know what George would find when he'd disappeared over the crest in search of

Nickie and Gina. It had felt like an age before he'd finally received George's text that Nickie and Gina were alive.

Glancing back at Nickie tied to the tree, he took a deep breath and settled himself. Though he was making her wait to accentuate his point and fuel her anticipation, the sight of her decimated car had rattled him. He needed a minute to regain his composure. Retrieving the riding crop she'd given him from under the driver's seat, he started back to her, carrying it in front of him as he approached.

Apprehension glimmered in her eyes.

Standing at her side and placing his lips at her ear, he began tapping the heart-shaped leather tongue across her naked backside.

"What do you have to say for yourself?"

"I shouldn't have taken off. I should have waited for Tyler and George to arrive. Gina said I shouldn't leave, but—"

"But you didn't listen," he scolded, slapping the leather heart in the center of her right cheek.

"Ow! No, Sir. I didn't listen."

He swatted her again, three times in rapid succession on the same spot.

"Keep going," he said calmly. "What else?"

"When I saw Gerald, I should have barricaded the barn door and waited for Tyler and George like Gina said. All I had to do was be patient for five minutes."

"Patience, there you have it," Beau said sternly, repeating the quick volley on the left cheek. "You will learn to be patient, young lady."

"Ow!, Oh, Sir. I'm sorry."

"Next time you're impatient you'll feel this crop again. What else?"

"Ooh, Sir, my ass is burning."

"What else?" he repeated, delivering several hard slaps with his hand.

"When we were driving up the hill Gina kept telling me to go back, but when we got to the top I couldn't turn around. The wind was rocking the car, and she warned me, she begged me not to drive up here, but I decided—"

"You decided you knew better," he scolded, cutting her off, "because Nicole Harris always knows better, Nicole Harris is smarter than anyone else, isn't she?"

"No," she bleated. "Okay, I used to think that way, but I don't anymore, I swear I don't."

Beau could see she was near tears, but not from the crop. Guilt and shame was surging through her.

"That's why you need to be punished, isn't it Nickie, for all those things you just talked about?"

"Yes, Sir."

"Ask me."

"Sir," she stammered, "please will you punish me for all those things, and, uh, for being so arrogant?"

"You've been arrogant?"

"Yes, Sir," she said softly, "I realize now I've been arrogant for a long time."

Leaning forward he kissed her neck, then turning her head, he dusted her lips.

"I'm real proud of you right now."

"You are?"

"You just admitted the truth about yourself."

"If I'm ever arrogant again, will you please, uh, handle it?"

"You can count on it. Are you ready to be properly disciplined?"

"Yes, Sir."

"Hold this between your teeth," he instructed, lifting the crop to her mouth.

As she bit down on the rolled leather rod, he smoothed his palm over her blotchy skin, then bounced his hand from cheek to cheek with hot, stinging smacks. She muttered muffled ouch's and ow's and wriggled against the tree, but when he landed the hard swats on the back of her thighs, she wailed in protest.

"Sir! Ooh! Ow! Sir! It hurts, please, I'm sorry, really, I'll behave!"

"I know you're sorry, Nickie," he declared, not missing a beat, "but you're bein' punished."

Landing several more for good measure, he returned his flattened palm to her bottom, delivering six hard slaps on each cheek.

"Catch your breath for a minute," he murmured, taking the crop from her mouth.

"Yes, Sir," she panted. "Thank you, Sir."

Stepping back, he studied her scarlet backside. It would still be tender the next day, and perhaps even the day after.

"Next time you feel like throwin' a tantrum or doin' something reckless, you'd best think about this moment. I won't hesitate to repeat it if I have to."

"Yes, Sir."

Laying the leather heart against her seat, he flicked it down with rapid-fire swats, making her squeal and squirm, then throwing it aside, he reached down to yank her panties from around her ankles, quickly untied her wrists, and brought her into his arms.

"Naughty Nickie," he purred. "You're punished properly. I love you, and you needed this."

"I know," she whimpered, "and I'm truly sorry."

He rocked her for several minutes, then slipped his fingers into her sex.

"Oh, girl, you are drippin'. I'm gonna take you home to our bed."

Moving his mouth to hers, he kissed her, but it was no ordinary brushing of the lips. It was an ardent, demanding passionate kiss. A kiss that took her breath away, that stirred her soul and sent a fresh wave of sexual heat through her pussy. A kiss that told her how deeply he loved her.

"I got our tests back yesterday," he whispered as they broke apart. "We're good to go."

"You mean…?"

"When we get home I'm gonna slide my naked cock deep inside you, baby, and I'm gonna screw your brains out."

"Ooh, did you have to say that? I don't think I can wait."

"I don't think I can either."

Releasing her, he hastily grabbed the sleeping bag that had fallen from the tree, flipped it out, and pulling her down with him, he rolled her onto her back.

"Ouch!"

"Was that your sore butt?" he asked with a wicked grin as he hastily unbuttoned her shirt. "Oh, darlin…no bra."

Diving his mouth to her breasts, he drew in her nipples and moved his fingers between her legs.

"Beau, I want you so much, so much I can hardly stand it."

Rising to his feet and quickly stripping, he kneeled between her legs, gripped her hips and jerked them into his pelvis.

"Ready for me?" he growled. "Really ready?"

"Yes, yes, please."

"You asked for it," he grunted, placing his cock at her entrance and plunging home.

Closing his eyes, he relished the feel of his naked member inside her warm, wet passage.

"You feel exquisite," she whimpered. "It's like heaven."

"It is heaven," he mumbled, and staying buried inside her, he lowered his weight gently on top of her body.

"Beau, I never want to leave here."

"You mean, here under the trees, or Lake Shimwah?"

"I mean here, under you, possessed by you. I belong here."

"Yeah, baby, you do."

Pressing his lips against hers, he began to stroke, his tongue dancing in her mouth as he thrust. Her muffled moans urging him on, he pounded her pussy with abandon. As his climax hovered, her fingers clawed his back, and he sensed she was on the edge. Her pussy suddenly pulsed against him, and without warning his climax took hold.

As the rippling waves sparked through his being, she shuddered through her orgasmic spasms. The crackling convulsions continued, until letting out their final cries, breathless and with their hearts pounding, their bodies fell limp.

A gentle breeze wafted around them, he slipped from her depths and fell beside her. Curling against him, she murmured his name.

"Yeah, babe," he panted, willing his heart to stop thundering.

"Can you do me a really big favor?"

"I reckon I can. What is it."

"Please don't let me mess this up."

A soft smile curling his lips, he rolled on his side and clutched her hair.

"Not a chance, darlin'," he growled, his smoky-blue eyes holding hers. "Not a chance."

# EPILOGUE

Nickie had been worried about her house. In spite of Beau's assurances, she was sure the Devil Wind would have caused significant damage. Finally convincing her it had survived remarkably well, she agreed to a visit.

"There was so much crap around the ranch," she said as they drove around the lake to her street. "I just couldn't face seeing it around my place."

"Nickie, your site might be on the side of a hill, but it's not as exposed. I wouldn't tell you it was okay if it wasn't."

"I know, I know. I guess I'm just now feeling ready to deal with things again."

"I can understand that," he said, reaching across the bench seat and taking her hand. "You went through hell. We all did."

"And most of it was my fault," she mumbled.

"Hey, that's done with. We all make mistakes, and sometimes they're big ones. It's time to move on, or should I spank you some more?"

"What? No!"

"Then forgive yourself. I have."

"I love you, Beau Champan."

"Glad to hear it," he said with a grin. "Look, the Hollister Hotel," he remarked as they passed.

"I can't believe how upset and miserable I was," she said with a sigh. "I had no idea how to get away from Gerald and my job. My whole life has changed thanks to you."

"You've got an angel on your shoulder."

"You're the angel on my shoulder," she said softly, leaning across to peck him on the cheek. "I'm actually happy."

"Honestly, Nickie, I never thought we'd end up like this," he murmured, shaking his head as he headed up her street. "If you hadn't stepped on that nail…"

"Best accident I've ever had," she said with a laugh.

"Ready to see what's what?"

"Yes, I'm fine. I have this awesome contractor who can fix any damage."

"Lucky girl, but like I said, there isn't any."

Driving slowly forward, she spied small branches littering the area, and stopping in front of the house, bits of paper and human trash lying on the ground.

"I thought this would be so much worse," she exclaimed, climbing from the truck. "I'm so relieved."

"I've gotta say I told you so," he declared with a chuckle and putting his arm around her shoulders. "Nickie, I've gotta surprise for you. Go into the house and check out the backyard, but don't turn around or come into the house until I tell you."

"Really? A surprise? What is it?" she asked with a wink. "Tell me. I won't breathe a word."

"Funny. Go on, and watch where you're walkin."

"Don't worry. I have no desire to end up with a sprained ankle, even if you are here to carry me away."

Waiting until she'd disappeared, he pushed the bench seat forward, and studied the items he needed to take into the house. Pulling out the picnic hamper Gina had packed, he placed the folded blanket on top, then the sleeping bag still rolled up from the day before. Lifting it out, he picked up his guitar and made his way to the kitchen area.

\* \* \*

"You really wanna pool, Nickie?" Beau asked, entering the back yard and hugging her from behind. "They can be a lotta trouble."

"That took you long enough."

"Good things are worth waitin' for," he murmured, kissing her on the cheek. "Back to my question. Are you sure you wanna pool?"

"I was just thinking I might like an oversized whirlpool tub instead, and a redwood deck."

"Sounds better. With all the foliage around here you'd be forever cleanin' a pool."

"Can I have my surprise now?"

"What happened to patience?"

"It doesn't count in a situation like this," she said with a giggle. "Please, Beau?"

"What am I gonna do with you?"

"Like you don't know the answer to that!"

"You're full of yourself today!"

"I'm happy!"

"Now that's an excuse I'll accept. Close your eyes and take my arm."

Guiding her through the house and into the kitchen, he stood her in the middle of the empty space.

"Okay, you can open them."

"Beau! My gosh!"

On the floor, a blanket was covered with a myriad of plastic containers offering a variety of delicious delights.

"Courtesy of Gina. Our first meal in your new home."

"This is fantastic. I can't believe it."

"And here's the first of three gifts from me," he said, lifting an envelope from his pocket.

"Three?"

"Yep."

Her pulse racing, she pulled out the card. The front showed an image of a western saddle sitting on a bale of hay, but opening it, she stared wide-eyed at a photograph of Trixie, and the two words written boldly above it.

**SHE'S YOURS.**

"Beau! You're not serious."

"I don't mess around with my horses."

"I can't believe it. I own a horse?"

"Yep. And it's legal. I've got the paperwork at the house. She's all yours. Every inch of her."

"Oh, my gosh. This is the best present ever. Thank you so much.

I'm thrilled. I'm beyond thrilled. I'll groom her and feed her and do everything."

"And you'll love every second. Ownin' a horse is something real special."

"I can feel it already."

"Now, uh, it's time for your next present."

His face had suddenly grown solemn, and reaching back into his pocket, he withdrew a small, black velvet box.

"You're a married woman, so, uh…dang it. I don't know how to say this. I'm not good at this stuff," he muttered, thrusting the box at her. "Open it."

Her heart racing even faster, and barely able to breathe, she lifted the lid to find a sparkling diamond ring on a shimmering silver chain.

"Beau…"

"Like I said, you're married, so I was thinkin', uh, Nickie, will you wear that around your neck?  When you're a free woman, if you want, and I want—"

"Yes, yes, yes," she exclaimed, cutting him off and throwing her arms around his neck.

"Sorry I made such a mess of that," he mumbled sheepishly.

"You didn't make a mess of anything," she said softly, pulling back and staring into his mesmerizing eyes. "It was perfect. Everything is perfect."

"You've made me real happy, sugar, and I've got one last gift."

"You've given me a horse and this amazing ring on a chain. What else could there possibly be?"

"Have a seat," he said, reaching behind the wall and picking up his guitar.

"You play?"

"A bit. Go ahead, sit down."

"This is the best day of my life," she declared, settling on the blanket.

"This is called, Naughty Angel," he said, shooting her a wink, and leaning back against a support beam, he began to strum.

I don't know where you came from,

I don't know who you are,
I admit to feelin' kinda strange
And I'm likin' it so far,

You're a different kinda woman,
With a different kinda love,
A different kinda something
A naughty Angel from above.

When you're nowhere in sight,
I still see you in my mind
I love feelin' you against me
Nickie, you're one of a kind.

You're a different kinda woman,
With a different kinda love,
A different kinda something
A naughty Angel from above.

You're runnin' fast and runnin' hard
Come run into my arms,
I'll lift you up when you're feelin' down,
And I'll keep you outta harm

Sometimes a woman needs a man
to step up and fight her fight.
Ain't no shame in that my love,
Stick with me, I'll make things right.

You're a different kinda woman,
With a different kinda love,
A different kinda something
A naughty Angel from above.

Sometimes it takes a miracle
to show us how we feel

Sometimes it takes a miracle
to show us just what's real
A miracle has touched my heart
A miracle, it's true,
A miracle that's blessed my life,
That miracle is you.


"Beau, I don't know what to say," she stammered, heat filling the back of her throat. "It was incredible. You're incredible."

As she rose quickly to her feet, he moved the guitar strap over his shoulder, rested the instrument carefully against the beam, then opened his arms.

"Come here, sugar."

"I'm the one that's blessed," she sniffled, falling against his chest. "Thank you. Thank you for everything."

"Nickie. you've brought so much light into my life."

"So much madness," she muttered, lifting her eyes.

"Yep, madness too, but way more joy, darlin'."

"Beau, there's just one thing," she said hesitantly. "This place. I mean, I'm so happy at the ranch, and when this house is finished..."

"I've been thinkin' along those lines myself."

"You have?"

"Sure. I'm not puttin' a cabin up on Flat Top now, no way. Did you know the Devil Wind is actually a wind wave?"

"A wind wave? No, I've never heard of it."

"That's what it is. Something to do with hot and cold air and the mountains, but regardless, the ranch doesn't have this," he said, gesturing to the stunning view of the lake and ragged peaks beyond. "We can live in both places, and if you ever get mad at me, you can run off up here."

"I'll never run away from you."

"I hope not, but if you ever do, at least you'll only be five minutes away when you come to your senses."

"You mean, when you come to yours!"

"Either way," he said with a grin, "five minutes is as far away from you as I ever wanna be. How does that sound to you?"

"Like everything else does. Perfect."

"Then how about we eat our lunch to celebrate, then officially christen this place."

"I'm sure I don't know what you mean," she quipped with a wink.

"A nap," he retorted. "The sleepin' bag's right over there."

"I have a much better idea," she whispered, circling his neck with her arms. "Why don't we christen the house first?"

"You know what I was just thinkin'? The Devil Wind is supposed to blow in trouble, and it tried, but it met up with an angel named Nickie. There's nothin' and no-one that can get the better of her. No-one except me."

"That's why I love you so fu—sorry, so darn much," she said with a happy sigh. "Who would have thought it?  An heiress and a cowboy contractor."

"Just like my song says. A miracle that's blessed my life. That miracle is you."

"And you cowboy. And you!"

**THE END**

*Dear Reader:*

*Thank you for buying this book. If you have a moment I would greatly appreciate your review. I constantly strive to bring you interesting and enjoyable content and your feedback is valued. Feel free to contact me at any time. I love to hear from readers. My email is: MagCarpenter@yahoo.com, and here are my social media links should you care to check them out.*
*My very best wishes,*
**Maggie**

https://www.MaggieCarpenter.com
https://www.facebook.com/MaggieCarpenterWriter
https://twitter.com/magcarpenter2